THE NEW
ADVENTURES OF
SINBAD THE SAILOR

SALIM BACHI

THE NEW
ADVENTURES
OF SINBAD
THE SAILOR

A NOVEL

Translated from the French by
Sue Rose

Pushkin Press
LONDON

Pushkin Press
71–75 Shelton Street, London WC2H 9JQ

Original text © Éditions Gallimard, Paris, 2010
English translation © Sue Rose 2012

The New Adventures of Sinbad the Sailor first published in French as
Amours et aventures de Sindbad le marin in 2010

This translation first published by Pushkin Press in 2012

This book is supported by the Institut Français
as part of the Burgess programme (www.frenchbooknews.com)

**INSTITUT
FRANÇAIS**

ISBN 978 1 906548 91 9

The extract from Sinbad's Fifth Voyage in Chapter XV was taken from
The Arabian Nights II: Sindbad and Other Popular Stories, translated by
Husain Haddawy. Copyright © 1995 by Husain Haddawy.
Used by permission of W.W. Norton & Company, Inc.

Also quoted is Rainer Maria Rilke's *Notebooks of Malte Laurids Brigge*,
translated from the German by William Needham
(http://www.archive.org/stream/TheNotebooksOfMalteLauridsBrigge/
TheNotebooksOfMalteLauridsBrigge_djvu.txt)

The author thanks the Centre National Du Livre for its support

Cover Illustration: Henry Rivers
© Henry Rivers 2012

Set in 10 on 13.5 Monotype Baskerville by Tetragon, London
Printed and bound by CPI Group (UK) Ltd

www.pushkinpress.com

For Amel

I

T HE DOG WAS VERY OLD now and its grey coat was covered in dark patches. It was walking in front of its master, feebly wagging its tail. Any memories of being a puppy had faded a long, long time ago. It had kept watch over its master, the Sleeper, who was at present disembarking from the boat; it had kept watch night and day and, Lord knows, those nights were long, and so were the days.

The town stretched out before them, white as the dawn that had broken over the sea. Once, the town had been called Algiers, but now its inhabitants called it Carthago, although this meant nothing to the traveller and his dog. In a different life, towns probably did not change so quickly, but those ancient memories of his were distant echoes that no longer bounced off the walls of the cave.

They walked down the gangway onto the quay, where men were jostling each other. The crowd swelled like a wave about to come crashing down onto a seawall in a storm, and the traveller didn't recognize a soul. His dog began whining, so he bent down and gently stroked its coat. They could then carry on pushing their way through the throng of men and women who looked nothing like those he'd known in his youth.

"Stop right there!"

A soldier had suddenly appeared before them.

Were they still at war, the man wondered, directing his question at the dog.

"Your papers!"

There was no other explanation: the nightmare, the terrible nightmare was still going on.

"Are you going to arrest me?"

The soldier stared at him as if he were mad. He noticed the dog and took a step back.

"Your passport, sir. Border police."

It was a strange kind of police force that behaved like an army in time of war, thought the man, rummaging in his jacket. He pulled out an old document creased by long years of use and handed it to the soldier, or policeman—he wasn't sure which.

"This isn't a passport!"

"That's all I've got."

"Apart from a dog."

The policeman turned the papers over in his hand, fingering them as if they were an ancient relic. He began leafing through and, as he turned the pages, his eyes grew as wide as two pale moons.

"Is there a problem, um… officer?"

He had hesitated before addressing him in this way. These sorts of scum could be very touchy, when they were not just plain stupid.

The other man removed his kepi and scratched his head.

"But this is a French passport! An old…"

"That's what it's supposed to be, officer."

"But it isn't Algerian; it isn't even a valid French passport. It dates from the war!"

"Is the war over?"

"It depends which one you mean. The first war ended in '62."

So there had been a second war. What a strange country this was, where one war followed hard on the heels of another, as if people had learnt nothing from history. Had he slept that long? Was his dog that old?

"Follow me!"

He hesitated.

"Both of you!"

———

THE SLEEPER might still have been young. He certainly looked it. If it weren't for that ancient, revolting dog which went everywhere with him, he could have passed for a man in his thirties. His clothes, however, could have been made a century ago. They were new but they looked as if they had come from a display cabinet in some museum, or one of those old shops you sometimes see in black and white films.

Although his black shoes still gleamed, they were gradually losing their shine as the boat brought him ever closer to what was Carthago, according to one of the other passengers, a young man whose occupation seemed to involve some kind of trading activity. He bought clothes at the other end of the world, transported them himself in large plastic bags and sold them at a market in Carthago. Why did he do such strange, tedious work?

"I'm a *biznessman*…"

He gestured to his bundle, which was spilling over with multi-coloured handkerchiefs, Italian shirt collars and an electric hairdryer.

"… a businessman! *Sinbad*. That's what they call me in my neck of the woods. Sinbad."

The dog raised its muzzle in his direction and yawned.

"That old mutt needs some shut-eye. Where on earth did you get it? It's older than Lalla Fatima, my grandmother!"

"Is she still alive?" asked the Sleeper, suddenly taking an interest in his fellow passenger's conversation.

"If you can call it living. She sleeps all day and spends her nights saying she'd be better off dead."

"Why?"

"She claims things were better before."

"And were they?"

"I'm a new man in a new country. They tell me that the town used to be called Algiers and is now called Carthago. So as far as I'm concerned, it's Carthago. They tell me things are better than before and I agree with those who shout this from their soapboxes. They're right, they've always been right... the war... all that stuff... it's all a pack of lies. Don't you think so, sir?"

The Sleeper wasn't thinking any more, he was daydreaming.

Carthago. It was a strange, musical name which sounded familiar to him. It was as if he'd woken from a nightmare to find himself trapped in one that was far worse, where even the name and appearance of the bloodstained city had changed; as if the city where they had shot partisans, slit women's throats and tortured children, the strange city he'd been forced to flee with his dog to take refuge in the mountains from the paratroopers, soldiers sent by Africa's generals, as if that city had finally acquired a name worthy of its reputation. *Carthago*.

"What does your grandmother think of the war?"

"Which war?"

Seeing the Sleeper's bewildered expression, the other man continued: "Oh, I see! You haven't moved on from the first! The great war... the one with the martyrs, the heroes, the evil paras..."

He began to laugh heartily, revealing a flash of teeth.

"Why are you laughing?"

"No reason, sir, no reason. I'm a new man in a new country. A *biznessman*. Sinbad the Traveller."

He had experienced war. He couldn't have said where or when. But what it was... that he knew only too well. It ran so deep that it felt like it was branded into his flesh. He only had to raise his arm or bend his back to feel it creeping painfully, viciously, through every fibre of his muscles to reach into the dark recesses of his soul. It marched in front of his eyes like the nightmare of a hundred nights, a thousand lives. Processions of prisoners filed past and the gates of the camps opened, spewing out corpses for Judgement Day. There were other monstrosities, other ghouls filling his fogged memory: cities ravaged by barbarian hordes; men, women and children confined in dark caves, crammed together in catacombs, imprisoned like rats, engulfed by flames, burned at the stake, huge living torches in the darkest parts of his soul. When he had awoken, he had found the dog watching over him, as dark and grey as the day he'd fallen asleep. Then he remembered the tale he'd been told by his grandmother, before she had been swallowed up by the darkness of death:

Dogs are seen as a blessing by the Faithful; he who treats them with kindness will receive it back hundredfold because they are the guardians of hell, my child, and yours will extinguish the flames threatening to devour your heart by plunging its tail in freezing water.

———

"WHERE ARE YOU FROM?"
"I don't remember."
The uniformed policeman scratched his head. He was somewhat bemused and mystified. Clearly, the Sleeper and his dog weren't your average travellers. He'd brought them to this prefabricated hut at the end of the quay. His colleagues didn't look best impressed when they came in, particularly by the dog with its grey coat, gaping mouth and putrid breath. Hell's teeth, didn't it stink! It was rotting away on the spot. How old was it, for goodness sake? Even the man, the animal's master since time began, didn't know.

Only the beast itself could have told them, but it just whined with its mouth open, wagging its tail and gazing at its master.

"Your papers aren't in order, sir. There's no date of birth. How old are you?"

The Sleeper stretched out his hands, turned them over and shrugged: he had no idea. Like a man waking from a long sleep who, in the morning, tries to gather his thoughts and piece together his memories.

"What are we going to do with this guy?"

A colleague who'd come over to the desk said, "Haven't we got enough on our plate as it is! The country is going to the dogs, no one would even recognize his own mother in this mayhem. One more won't make any difference."

"But his papers."

The other man started laughing.

"Leave it out. Everything in this country has gone up in smoke! That's identity-theft for you. Show me a boss round here who gives a damn about an ID card or passport! What are they good for, anyway?"

"Travelling."

"Into the arsehole of hell! Death without a destination! Who needs passports? Kids build rafts so they can die at sea… pass-ports… it's a bloody joke… We get an illegal immigrant for once, and you want to give him a hard time?"

The Sleeper asked, "Children build rafts?"

"Yes, Mister Nowhere Man. Kids… shipbuilders. They build shipwrecks with their bare hands out of a few planks and some tyres! They run aground or earn themselves a fine death at sea under the watchful eyes of the Spanish, Italian or Maltese coastguard."

"Some of them survive, don't they?"

"If you can call it that… walking skeletons… they're herded into camps, fed, nursed back to health, then sent back to us so they can get lost at sea all over again."

"Why are these children running away?"

The policemen stared at him as if he'd said something stupid. One of them handed back his old passport and the other spat on the ground.

"It's a long story, sir."

He was in no hurry.

The dog had actually fallen asleep at his feet. A blessing in itself: with its mouth shut, the air was easier to breathe. The fact that it was no longer wagging its tail also meant that any decaying particles fell straight to the ground instead of being sprayed into the stifling air of the shack.

The authorities had been promising to build them proper offices for the past twenty years. They had been dumped at the end of the quay behind a disused boathouse and promptly forgotten. When an illegal immigrant like this man and his dog passed through their hands, they grilled him with no particular malice, away from prying eyes. If it was someone suspicious, like a terrorist coming back to Carthago to try out his pyrotechnical skills, they handed him over to the real police, the bad police who kept the basements of their police stations so spick and span. At first glance, this man and his dog were just a couple of harmless nutcases.

"Sir, you need a name, it doesn't matter what it is." He pointed to his colleague: "He's Achilles; I'm Patroclus. Or Castor and Pollux, or Thomson and Thompson, who cares… you could be… wait, let me think… No One! Yes, No One."

The dog shook itself and its fleas.

"Aha, I had you fooled, didn't I! You thought we were complete halfwits. But I can assure you we've come a long way since Independence. We cops are no fools. We even have publishers who produce guidebooks to the town."

He opened a drawer, rummaged around and took out a book. He smacked it against his hand to remove the dust, then handed it to him.

15

———

FLASHES OF MEMORY like lightning in the dark. He had lived several lives; but this was probably just another dream. How long had he slept? How many years? Was he suffering from amnesia? No. The only explanation was that he'd been outside time for part of his life. Unsatisfactory. He still had these blinding memories: heightened emotions, lost loves, lengthy parades, headlong flights. Had the dog always been with him? He wasn't sure. The animal had turned up later; he'd woken up beside it. But was it his? For the present it was. The ancient creature turned its head towards him and rubbed its muzzle against his leg. In return, he stroked its flank. He had the strange sensation that his hand was touching something else, as if his fingers were sinking into the soft flesh of a decaying carcass.

"So those bastards let you go! Oh, if you only knew... they held me for five hours... they unpacked everything... my bags, my things... all jumbled up... all over the floor. I tried telling them I was Sinbad, but it was no good, they wouldn't listen! Those bastards. That reminds me, what name did God give you, my humble friend?"

"My name is No One."

"He had a sense of humour. You don't come across that every day. What about your dog?"

"Dog."

"Those customs officers, those policemen! They are legion, you know, as it says in the book of the Christians."

"You mean the Gospels?"

"We call it the *Injil*, which is how it translates into Arabic. My friend... No One... do you speak the language of the seventh-century Qurayshites the way our Lord and Master spoke it, may

16

the prayers of God and man be upon Him, our dearly beloved of angels and fools, our prophet Mohammed? Because if you don't speak that ancient language forgotten by all, you won't survive here. If you can find the exact equivalent in colonial French, the language of the collective rape of our virgins, then… you might be mistaken for an honest citizen of Carthago."

Sinbad began laughing so hard that he dropped his bag which spilled its contents over the quay.

The port looked like a prison. Metal bars as far as the eye could see. He had to get out of this cage! Dog began growling; his master tapped him on the back; the growling stopped. Incandescent lava flowed beneath the vast blue sky; the air was liquefying like molten metal. Dog turned his gaping mouth to the sea to drink in cooler air. An occasional breeze brushed over his ears, then disappeared, leaving only that hellish heat beneath a brutal sun. But they had to keep going, they had to escape from that cooking pot and make their way to the heights of Carthago. They followed Sinbad. He knew the way. When they arrived at the gate, he turned to them.

"*Willkommen daheim*! I've had to learn the languages of the world. Every single one. My travels often take me to places you wouldn't imagine. We even trade with China: 'the workshop of the world'. I read that once in the paper. That's what they say now. The workshop of the… they even make Moroccan slippers! I have to buy them there to sell them to our housewives. I've seen African merchants buy masks and fetishes to sell at home. *Made in China*. Masks straight out of hell. I'll never get used to it. It beggars belief! All those countries, all those customs, all those different ways of eating, dressing, loving… I shall never thank God enough for giving me eyes and legs and for ensuring that I was born in this country where life isn't easy."

"Where are we going?"

"Back to my house! It isn't far. It's just a taxi ride away."

Then he looked at Dog and said, "He'll never be allowed in the car. People don't like animals here. Or men… and, as for women and children, you can forget it."

"Why?"

"There's no room, Mister No One. Can you believe it, we've run out of parking spaces in this life! We've had to go running to the Chinese, yet again, to build a few more apartment blocks to provide housing for all the people reproducing furiously under the gaze of God. Worse than cats. Or rabbits. So women and children are cursed by men… they take up too much room. You can understand it, can't you? Sometimes, on a boat, when we're far away, I have the strangest thoughts… terrible thoughts… I can't tell anybody about them, because they make me feel so ashamed."

"What sort of…"

"…all these wars haven't even solved our problem of overcrowding. Get my drift?"

"Not really."

"I'm not expressing myself very clearly, I realize that. Well then, let me be frank and honest. I think honesty is a quality people often lack."

He set down his bag and looked at the Sleeper and his dog.

"No One, are you old enough to hear a few home truths?"

Dog yelped and stretched out his muzzle; he stared at Sinbad as if he represented some kind of threat. It was as if that dog had sprung from some terrifying hellhole: Dog's age was even more of a mystery than that of his master. The fact that he was old did nothing to alleviate anyone's uneasiness. His grey coat, long emaciated legs, protruding tongue and shortness of breath might have misled some into believing that the beast was on his last legs. But first impressions can be deceptive: this dog might be ageless, but he certainly wasn't defenceless or weak. The animal remained true to his primary calling.

———

T HEY FOUND A TAXI that would take animals, although only in the boot; the dog would never survive being locked in there in the scorching heat. The boot was air-conditioned, just like the car, insisted the driver, who'd had a lot of experience with journeys made under duress.

"I worked for the military police! They gave me a taxi licence for violences rendered. Now I'm my own boss."

"What's your name?" asked Sinbad.

"Charon. Round here, they pronounce it *Karun*. I transport anyone who wants to take a seat in my ferry!"

He began laughing as if he'd just told the funniest joke ever. Sinbad squirmed on the back seat, feeling uncomfortable. In the front, the Sleeper watched the road as if the conversation had nothing to do with him. He watched Carthago stretching away in every direction at each junction, the sea sparkling like a carpet of rubies.

"You're an honest man, sir," said Sinbad. "Why else would you feel the need to tell us that you used to work for the secret police?"

"I give you Charon's word, I never lie to my passengers. It's not the done thing in this job. They're nice guys who usually don't say a word and accept their fate. Occasionally, it's more difficult… they aren't all like you. I've had some… who didn't understand what was happening to them."

"Are you talking about your old job?" asked the Sleeper.

Sinbad was sweating despite the air-conditioning.

"Mr Charon, don't be angry with him," said Sinbad. "He has no idea how things are done. The questions he's asking aren't important."

The driver stopped his taxi. He took his time before turning round to face Sinbad.

"He doesn't know how things are done but, like every other son of a bitch who gets in my taxi, he does deserve some kind of explanation. I've nothing to hide. I've worked for the military police, military security, the army and the cops, and I'm proud of it! Do you have a problem with that?"

Sinbad said nothing and slumped even lower. He would have liked to disappear into the folds of the upholstery.

"I obeyed orders!" yelled the driver, starting the taxi again and revving the engine with a deafening roar. "I cleared the town of its troublemakers. I put them in my boot, like your dog, sir, and I drove them to basements from which they never emerged again. They were all butchered, one by one. When I use the word 'butchered', that has nothing to do with what really went on. They used the same techniques as the paratroopers in their time. They had even improved on some of them. There were rumours that they had perfected their investigative methods."

Dog began growling in the boot. There was the occasional loud thump as if the animal were trying to escape by throwing itself against the metal body of the car. His master was gazing at the sea, which faithfully kept pace with them, as memories flooded his mind. When Dog began howling, he shouted at him to be quiet. Dog fell silent as death.

"Your dog is well-trained. My passengers weren't as obedient as that. You could hear them shouting. Some of them soiled the boot. I had to clean everything up afterwards."

He continued, thoughtfully, "It's a hard job. But you get used to it, don't you? The worst, sir… Here, take this…"

He leant forward, opened the glove compartment and pulled out a handgun.

"A Beretta!"

The driver lifted the barrel into the sunlight and the weapon glinted strangely.

20

"I had to kill them sometimes because they were making too much noise. Then I'd take them to Cape Matifu."

The name rang a bell. As if Cape Matifu were the exact place where he and Dog had emerged from the Cave. People said that the Sleepers had been able to rest there after being driven out of Ephesus. But those were just ancient legends.

"That was before the town became as intolerable as it is now! At night, it was a very quiet, very pleasant place, where life was good. I'd open the car boot and fire at random. I'd empty the whole cartridge. Occasionally, some of them kept groaning—a bit like your dog, sir. Then I'd drag out the bodies and set fire to them. You wanted me to be honest, didn't you, Mr Sinbad?"

Sinbad didn't say a word. He remembered Cain and his brother Abel and the first drop of blood shed.

The taxi continued on its way, as silent as the grave.

"BOULEVARD CHE GUEVARA; Rue Ben M'Hidi; Place de l'Emir Abdelkader…"

Still in the taxi, Sinbad was identifying the places they passed to his guest, and Carthago was coming to life in the traveller's mind. He certainly remembered boulevards, streets and squares, but the names had changed, arrayed now in death's ceremonial livery.

What had become of them? Ben M'Hidi, Che Guevara, Abdelkader… they were all dead now.

The Sleeper thought back to the years he'd spent with them, sharing hopes and dreams that, although dead and gone, lingered on in the minds of the living. Had he fallen asleep yesterday after Ben M'Hidi had been arrested, or the day before yesterday after Emir Abdelkader had been captured? Had he gone into exile in Damascus to spend the rest of his days with the wise old man, amid prayers in the Umayyad Mosque? Perhaps he had died in Bolivia, trapped in the jungle, abandoned on the revolutionary path? Or, going back even earlier, was he washing Jugurtha's feet, kissing Jesus's feet, accompanying the Prophet on his hegira? He might be Jewish, Roman or Berber; he might have walked with the Arabs alongside their caravans; crossed the Atlantic on a slave ship; perished in the silver mines of Mexico; prostrated himself before the Kaaba or kissed the wall of the Temple in Jerusalem. Because it had been an eternity since he'd fallen asleep beside his companions, guarded by that ageless dog as the centuries accumulated.

One question, though, kept pestering him like a persistent mosquito: why had he woken up here? And where had the six other Sleepers gone? To which countries or continents? What were they going to tell mankind? Why had he been the only one to inherit Dog? Or had the creature divided itself up so as to accompany each Sleeper, the way that the monstrous beast of ancient legend had been cursed with several heads and thousands of fangs? Seven hideous mouths gaped and growled on five continents: they were about to devour the light.

Carthago suddenly appeared at the bend of a street and tumbled down to the contracting sea like a dirty carpet. As if God had decided to punish men by giving them an untameable mistress who would claim their lives aboard galleons crammed with gold and silver. But the time of the armadas had passed and he was the only one who remembered them. The present has no desire to recall anything of the past: it gropes around in the half-light, building a ghostly reality out of indistinct fragments.

"Being honest would mean..." continued Sinbad, as if also waking from a dream.

"No reasons, no honesty, just brute force," broke in the taxi driver, looking more and more like a gargoyle. "That's all those bastards understand."

"Nonsense!"

"Shut your mouth, you pedlar of crap! You bloody second-hand-clothes salesman, drug-dealer, pimp… You and your sort stick your cocks into the whorehouses of the world and come back to unload your diseases on us. All the hairdressers in Carthago have AIDS because of you. And you come here and talk to us about honesty?"

"You've murdered anyone who had a soul. There's no one left except creatures like you… gorgons, ghouls, the Devil…"

The driver stopped his taxi. He leant forward and, shaking, reached for the glove compartment.

"Are you looking for something?" asked the Sleeper.

"What, you… you…"

The Sleeper had the Beretta in his hand. God knows what magic he'd used to spirit it away. The driver wasn't in the least surprised. Maybe he'd never put it back in the glove compartment. Maybe, being stupid and arrogant, he'd actually given it to that strange man himself. He heard the click of the gun being cocked.

"I'm not the one who… I'm as innocent… as the sheep or the lamb, that's right, as the Eid lamb!" The gargoyle was backing down. It entreated Sinbad, "Tell him… I'm innocent… as innocent…"

"As the *Agnus Dei.*"

Sinbad was satisfied with this response. Anyway, he felt as though he couldn't relax unless he was continually on the run from something in this town. Who knows? If more men had shared his new friend's moral fibre, he might never have set foot on a ship again.

"Get out of the car," said the Sleeper.

The driver opened the door.

"Don't even think of trying to get away. I've never fired a gun, but I'm sure I'll manage to hit you at this distance."

One by one they climbed out of the car and, as if by some miracle, they found themselves in the middle of nowhere. Carthago was an enchantress with all kinds of solitary places up her sleeve, vast stretches of land where death could roam free.

"Open the boot!"

The Sleeper kept the gun trained on the taxi driver. The animal snarled, snuffled and growled even louder. It sounded as if it had grown during the journey. Dog had turned into the famished Creature waiting for sustenance and reward.

"Please, I'm begging you…"

"Open it!"

Dog was also thinking. He recognized his master. By his smell. He even gave him a name. Ooourugarri, Ooourugarri the Sleeper. The name referred to the strange smell of his master, Ooourugarri. Dog wasn't hungry any more, Dog had eaten his fill. His master had given him permission to eat. Ooourugarri was a good master when he wasn't sleeping. Ooourugarri had slept a long time with his friends, the other six. At the beginning of Time, Dog had kept watch over the Seven Sleepers. Then the Sleepers had awoken, taken a name and Dog had divided himself to follow each man as he left. Ooourugarri was the last Sleeper and Dog had divided himself one last time to follow him. When the last Sleeper, whose name was unpronounceable, awoke, the Prophecy would be fulfilled, according to the legend that Dog did not know but sensed in the depths of his animal memory. And: the weighing out on that day will be just; as for those whose measure of good deeds is heavy, they shall be deemed successful. And as for those whose measure of good deeds is light, they shall be deemed to have made their souls suffer loss because they disbelieved in Our communications. Thus spoke Time; and Ooourugarri was the last Sleeper. He was the one who was to announce the Coming of the Messiah. He was a good master, thought Dog. A master who stroked him and fed him when he was hungry. And Dog had eaten so well that he felt heavy now, and happy that he could rest here. After he had eaten, Dog had walked in front of Ooourugarri and his new friend, the Traveller, for a long time. He talked a lot. Dog didn't understand all of it. But he knew that the Traveller was a good man. Dog would not eat him; Ooourugarri, his master, would not allow it. Dog didn't eat often, so Dog was often hungry. Very hungry. Ravenously hungry. As hungry, in Dog's mind, as he had been in the morning light when he had divided himself and had first emerged from the Cave where he had been watching over the Seven Sleepers. Now Dog could rest in the house of the Traveller, the man who talked and talked and talked, but who was a Good Man and who wouldn't be good food for Dog; not as good as that Bad Man who had locked him in the iron cave, not nearly as good. In the Cave, he would often burrow in the soil to feed on those dark balls that he managed to dig out of the dust. That wasn't good food for Dog, but Dog couldn't leave the Cave, and Time had forbidden him to eat the Seven Sleepers. Poor Dog.

———

THE SLEEPER AND SINBAD were strolling along Boulevard Che Guevara in the light reflected by the sea. It was very hot and the sun was impassively casting a fiery glow over the streets of the town and the people walking about. A sea breeze blew between the columns and lifted the dresses of the veiled women. The Sleeper didn't recognize this strange uniform. He remembered the women of Carthago covering themselves with a white haik and wearing a gag over their nose and mouth, an ancient forerunner of the surgical mask. Only their arms and legs were bare, ornamented with bracelets of gold, or of copper for the women of more modest means. The more provocative women flaunted their bare legs and wiggled their behinds like dancers, while the older women could stare brazenly at the men passing by without any fear. Most of these men, inflexible as justice itself, were also badly dressed, wearing neither their old corsair costumes nor the restrictive French uniform of tight shirt collars and straight trousers. They either wore jeans teamed with an ill-matched T-shirt or opted for Commander Massoud's Afghan-style garments with a long beard hanging onto their chest which, in the case of the hairiest men, stuck out all over the place as if defying the fundamental laws of Newtonian physics.

The white veil had then disappeared and been replaced by a long, plain, black dress that followed the contours of the body more closely and was topped off by a headdress covering the hair and ears, like an astronaut's helmet with an oval opening, which made the face look longer, like a marrow. It had to be more practical, thought the Sleeper, much more practical than the white sack of Algiers or the black sack of Constantine, the two colours of mourning which had imprisoned women. But why didn't they walk around with nothing on their heads, their hair blowing in the wind, and their legs bare? Had women still not freed themselves from their chains? Some of them dared to walk in the light, beneath God's sun, with uncovered heads, eager buttocks and slender ankles: goddesses and bewitching sirens whom he liked to watch weaving between the arcades and the sea, which cast silvery flashes on the walls, like a vast broken mirror.

"Square Port-Said!" announced Sinbad, who was taking his role as tourist guide seriously.

But the Sleeper knew the square which sloped up towards the Opera House. In his time—although memory can be unreli-able—it was Square de la République; then, later on, Square Aristide-Briand; and then Square Bresson during the war, the one that had seen Carthago give birth to Square Port-Said on gaining independence after a long and painful labour.

Hadn't he attended the inauguration of the Opera House, now the National Theatre, in 1853, under French rule, then watched it burn down twenty years later? Hadn't he seen it rebuilt, just before the Great War, in 1914? Time had enabled him to go up on deck and sail through the centuries, while his companions slept in that dark Cave guarded by a dog which was now by his side. Or else, more likely, all those events had been a dream: the Great War, the millions of deaths. The Sleeper had even borne arms in the colonies to defend the Empire, like all those natives who'd had their faces painted for a foreign war, then sailed off for another, even more violent, conflict, as if the Demiurge, that entity who'd fashioned Dog, Death and Time, had set the stage for this bloody tragedy in which he was both the Spectator and the Tempter.

In the Sleeper's mind, the Opera House, overlooking this square with its palm trees, symbolized both a stage where the tragedy *La Kahina* had been performed in Arabic in 1954, on the eve of the Algerian war, and the world that witnessed every kind of horror: an endless *danse macabre* shook the stage and carried off the souls of the dead seated in the ancient auditorium, who always stood up at the end of the show to applaud the actors, clacking their bones and jaws.

"Did you know, my dear sir, that a play called *La Kahina* was put on in this theatre in 1954, a century after it was built. No more celebrations. What a premonition! Especially when you know that the Berber warrior-woman was the Joan of Arc of her day and spent her whole life fighting the Arab invaders!"

Sinbad had the irritating habit of exclaiming loudly all the time, which startled Dog, who bared his fangs without making a sound.

They were sitting on a bench in Square Port-Said in the shade of a giant Latan palm, whose outspread fronds sheltered the two men and Dog from the fierce heat of the sun.

Further down the square, the waves cast needles of light over the sky, and they could hear the heady lament of the surf, a hypnotic refrain which soothed Sinbad, transporting his thoughts to shores where he had once anchored. He saw again those enchanting cities: Granada and Cordoba, Rome and Florence and, farther away, Damascus and Bosra. Finally Paris, whose brilliance was now on the wane.

Sinbad was just about to say something when the sky and sea exploded into pieces. The world was reduced to sound and fury.

Ooourugarri had been felled along with the tree. And Sinnnbaaad. Dog hadn't moved. He breathed in the smell of blood and cordite. Dog thought it was a good smell. Dog bounded over to his master and licked his face for many minutes. Ooourugarri opened his eyes and looked around, just as he'd done after his long sleep in the Cave. He dusted down his clothes and stood up. Hundreds of branches and leaves fell to the ground in pieces, like a hail of grapeshot. All around, people were screaming and crying, and Dog liked that. His hunger thundered in his belly like a thousand guns, even more powerful than the explosion that had scattered the bodies of around ten men, women and children, but which had only skimmed the surface of his mind like a mundane signal, a bell summoning him to his quarry. If his master hadn't held him back, he would have pounced on the wounded and dead and would have devoured them, appeasing the monster roiling in his stomach. Mut the divine was also standing there in the light, the goddess who had claimed her due and was waiting to capture other souls. Dog had no soul. He had a stomach. That was enough. He also had a master, Ooourugarri, who was leaning over Sinnnbaaad, the man who smelled of salt and sweat, and was trying to rouse him. If Sinnnbaaad were dead, Dog could eat him at last. Dog hoped his master, Ooourugarri, would let him cleanse the world of this person who would thwart their plans. Dog was sure of it, his master cared for Sinnnbaaad, and that wasn't right. There was no need for love. In the Cave, he had waited without love for his masters to wake and to divide himself whenever one of them walked the world's path again. He had been the faithful guardian of their sleep without love. That was Dog's mission, a faithful guardian without a memory. The Demiurge denied memory. He thought up a world, shaped it, then destroyed it at will when it was time to begin again. Dog was convinced it was time for destruction. If not, why had Ooourugarri, the last of the Sleepers, finally awoken? And why had faithful Dog divided himself for one last time? Could Sinnnbaaad thwart the Demiurge's Plan? Could he prevent the complete destruction that crawled in Dog's stomach like a ravenous hunger and was only waiting for the tolling of the bell to set Dog on the world to devour it? It had to be here, in this town where blood was being shed, where the dead called to the dead, where children lost their eyes, became deaf and orphaned, that the destruction, followed by the recreation, of the World would begin, with him, Dog, and his master, Ooourugarri. Dog hoped Sinnnbaaad was dead, dead at last. Dog could no longer put up with his prattling. He could no longer tolerate the Sailor's endless babble.

———

S INBAD CAME TO, his head cradled in the Sleeper's hands which were as hard as stone. All around, the small square was in chaos, men and women lying among scattered branches. Rivulets of blood trickled among the leaves, staining the stone and pooling in small crimson lakes. Ambulances were parked in front of the theatre and stretcher-bearers, assisted by a few passers-by, were lifting up the wounded, strapping them onto gurneys and pushing them hastily into their vehicles. These then drove away again, their axles, crumpled metal and sirens making a din, while a line of taxis formed to pick up more of the dead or dying. Screams, tears and laments rose up in the warm air which still caressed the trees, ruffled the leaves and caused the branches to sway, while Sinbad explained the reason for this commotion, his ragged breathing a little affected. The Sleeper gazed, as cool as his hands, at the sight of this violence which was so familiar to him and which had remained unchanged since the dawn of time. Naturally, techniques had been perfected, and now, instead of smoking out innocent victims after herding them into caves, they blew them up—which saved a good deal of time.

"Does this happen often?"

"Every day," said Sinbad. "Every day some lunatic detonates a device in the middle of a crowd. It's a national sport. A local custom. Don't worry, you'll get used to it. You can get used to anything."

The Sleeper moved his head although, as usual, it was impossible to tell whether he was agreeing or disagreeing. His dog, whose mouth was watering at the smell, could not stand still: it was growling, whining, pricking up its ears and drooling, as if about to rush for its bowl.

"Anyway, no one gives a damn. It doesn't even make the papers these days. And the dead aren't likely to make a fuss, are they?"

"What about the wounded? The orphans?"

"They were in the wrong place at the wrong time."

Sinbad wasn't a cynic. He had barely woken from that hideous dream in which he'd almost lost his life. He felt as though he were facing the darkness alone. He felt weak and fragile. This was the very reason why he'd run away from the disaster that descended on Carthago with monotonous regularity. The city burned daily, and every day it was something different. He also understood why the kids of the town, tired of living in this hell, had begun to build the rafts that became such terrible shipwrecks. By night, they left the lights of Carthago behind and, at the water's edge, constructed their small craft, like opium dreams. They built their shipwrecks because no one let them pick up the threads of their lives.

"Doesn't anybody stop them?" asked the Sleeper.

"They leave at dawn. Like I did, a long time ago."

———

T HE GAWPING ONLOOKERS, alarmed by this strange group, parted to let them through. Dog had regained his strength, as if reinvigorated by the events of the day, his encounter with the taxi driver and the attack on Square Port-Said: he was energized by the smell of carnage flowing through him like an electric current. The dead bodies, the screams, the men lying face down on the pavement, the uprooted trees, the wailing of sirens, the coming and going of ambulances, had changed his psyche, arousing terrible instincts, connecting new nerve endings, producing new organs and forming new muscles. Despite appearances, Dog was far more formidable than the animal domesticated by man fifteen thousand years earlier. The Sleeper's companion was a creature fashioned in the bowels of the earth, a diabolical creation, assuming that the Demiurge did indeed exist and that the universe represented form without purpose. Our world, illuminated by Nothing, was a Cave whose walls showed terrible images that had men mimicking actions they didn't understand, while governed by urges they concealed under the guise of reason. God had no place in this macabre performance. Wherever the world was, God wasn't there. He was somewhere beyond the spheres and galaxies that had been launched into space after the first spark like missiles. God had died at that moment and had been replaced by Fate.

Sinbad had been drifting off course ever since he'd met the stranger and his dog, ever since that night when he'd gone over to them on the boat as it was nearing Carthago. He should never have met them. He was the complete opposite of the Sleeper and his dog. One side represented life, youth and love, and the other was the complete negation of these qualities. Sinbad was being contaminated by the gloomy presence of the Sleeper, as if darkness were threatening to claim him too. His story was no longer of any interest, although he would still insist on telling it. His life's adventures, his voyages and his women signified nothing; he would describe them to the Sleeper, whose ear was like a bottomless well in which words and emotions dissolved and disappeared. He'd tell him about his voyage to Italy, Syria and, finally, his return in the midst of war, but he didn't care about any of that now—his life had been slowly ebbing away since he'd been in the company of the Sleeper and Dog, whose dark mission frightened him.

Apart from him, who would give a damn about the stories?

Who these days took the time to read a book or listen to a man inventing his life? *Realism* had become the boring byword in this fiendishly modern world. Even the great massacres were scientific achievements, programmes and statistics. Homer and Scheherazade belonged to a lost race. No one would ever bewitch the world again. Someone had to acknowledge this, thought Sinbad, on the verge of tears. Dog's coat was gleaming in the sun and his mouth opened to breathe in the warm air blowing between the buildings. Sinbad felt that the oven-like heat around him was being sustained by the animal's fetid breath. The creature was part of the natural order, like the ground and the sun, or the primordial ocean that had witnessed the birth of life. Sinbad and the Sleeper stopped in front of the Grande Poste for a breather. The sun, now at its zenith, was baking the asphalt. It was two o'clock in the afternoon. The sky was white as molten metal.

II

B UILT in the eighteenth century, at the end of the rule of
the Sublime Porte, the house Sinbad shared with his grandmother, Lalla Fatima, boasted the magnificence of a bey's palace
combined with the old-fashioned charm of a family home. It was
three storeys high and arranged around a patio with a murmuring
fountain. The villa's rooms had balconies overlooking the fountain's
shivering pool. In summer, the women used to stretch out on its
broad ledge, legs splayed, and slowly fan themselves while their
energetic children played war games.

This palace, now occupied solely by Sinbad and his grandmother,
was the only one left in the Kasbah that had not fallen into ruin.

The two men and the dog had walked through the ancient
Citadel at night. The Sleeper had been able to observe the true
extent of the destruction. This wayward and idiosyncratic town,
which had survived the invincible armada, the madness of
Charles V, the capture of Oran, the influx of the French armies,
the encirclement by colonial troops, partition, the Anglo-American
invasion, as well as twenty or thirty earthquakes which would have
made the Lisbon Earthquake look like trampoline practice—in
other words, five centuries of bitter conflict, bloody wars and
all kinds of upheaval—would not survive the following decade,
even though it looked set to be one of the most peaceful periods
ever experienced by this damned country. The Citadel which, in

its immaculate whiteness, had once been the pride of Carthago, was now an image of its shame, its hidden face an exact likeness of its decline. All that remained of those ancient lanes where Barbarossa's corsairs had once lived were isolated sections of wall, ruined interiors and roofless villas opening onto nothing: Pompeii was beautiful in comparison.

Time caught hold of the Sleeper again and memories washed over him. He again saw the images from his nightmare. He was walking around Hiroshima, through the rubble of the Twin Towers, and in Dresden after the bombing, where women and children had been caught in shelters like rats in a trap. He became one with spectres from all the holocausts, the concentration camp prisoners, the mountains of bones and skulls piled high by the hordes of Genghis Khan, the Killing Fields, the lines of prisoners led to torture in all the cellars and basements of this vast world, whose fearsome beauty, he realized in a final epiphany, was nothing but a Guantanamo with mod cons.

"Welcome to our home," said Sinbad. "Please come in… don't stand on ceremony."

———

T HE WOMAN looked older than the Sleeper's dog. She was crouching on a rug, her back supported by a multitude of velvet cushions embroidered with gold thread which glittered in the dim light. Her face was deeply lined and it was impossible for him to make out behind the wrinkles the young woman she had once been.

Lalla Fatima was sitting there like an ancient deity, a vestal virgin from some sacred, yet forgotten, cult.

"You're the man foretold in the prophecy," she said in a voice which sounded far too young for her mummified appearance.

"I'm No One."

She recoiled, which did not escape his notice, despite the poor light in the tapestried room. Generations of women weavers had stretched and cut these threads every day, as if in reality stretching and cutting the ties that bound men to life. The Sleeper was well aware that, one day, when death claimed this woman, she would be buried in one of these hangings.

"Why do you have that dog with you?" she asked in the same soft voice.

"It's the Guardian."

Sinbad shifted restlessly, vaguely anxious.

"The Guardian?"

"Of the two worlds," replied the Sleeper. "It was he who guarded our sleep and prepared for our awakening."

"You're leaving something out," continued the old woman. "The prophecy is clearer than that."

"What does it say, Lalla Fatima?" asked Sinbad.

The old woman ignored the question and fixed her blue eyes on the Sleeper's face.

"You've come to see what the men of this country have done, haven't you? You're here for Judgement Day. My father often spoke to me about it. He said: 'On the day that every soul shall find gathered together what it has done of good and what it has done of evil, it shall wish that between it and that evil there were a long passage of time.' Has that Day come when we should fear you?"

The Sleeper could not reply. He would have liked to understand what had brought him here. Not to this room, but to Carthago, which he had once loved so dearly and which now looked like nothing on earth. He wondered if he might not be the plaything of the Demiurge, who had brought him back to life to torment him. Or maybe he was just an amnesiac who had been forced to board a boat so that he could be sent back to his people, like one of those illegal immigrants picked up on the streets of Paris,

35

Rome or London? He had probably set sail from here at the end of the war to work in a factory, on a building site or in a barren field. He had lived alone, without a wife or children, an unarmed soldier in an economic war, a modern-day serf. That was probably the root of the problem: he was a former slave sent home in the evening of his life. But no one, in that situation, would have saddled himself with a fearsome dog.

———

S INBAD HAD PREPARED a room for the Sleeper on the first floor, under the arches and the slender columns of this former cloister, often infiltrated by the protective rays of the sun. That evening, the full moon cast a spell over the Turkish house that was home to two lonely people, separated by age and history.

Sinbad had met him on the boat coming back from Marseilles. He'd seen him leaning against the ship's rail, gazing at the city's skyline with a distracted, yet determined, expression. After that, he'd noticed the pitiful dog, all skin and bones and receding gums. Since then, the animal had perked up. Its ears were cocked and its eyes had brightened during the day. Its muscles were now bulging beneath its coat.

Sinbad had no reason to question his first impression of the Sleeper on the boat as it drew nearer to Carthago which, in a stroke of genius or folly, had been excavated from the past by one man, the way you might unearth a treasure or an ancient mummy and show it to the world, or exhibit the tattered rags of a defeated people or the soiled garments of a rape victim.

Sinbad sat down before his guest and began telling him the true story of his life:

"I, Sinbad, was a happy man. The son of one of the most successful merchants in Carthago, I inherited a substantial fortune on

36

my father's death. I spent all my time living it up with my friends. I thought this way of life would never end. I lived like this for a long time until I finally came to my senses and saw the error of my ways. Then I realized that I'd squandered my fortune and that my position had deteriorated. One day, I had nothing left and the prospect of being poor made me tremble with fear. As the great King Solomon once said, 'These three things are better than the other three: the day of death is better than the day of birth; a live dog is better than a dead lion; and the grave is better than want.'

"So, with some twenty other people, I boarded a fishing vessel and set out to conquer Europe, where I thought I'd make my fortune, then come back to live with my kin as I had before.

"We were packed together in the boat, like animals, with hardly any food. Each passenger had paid a fare equivalent to a year's wages. Sometimes their family clubbed together to pay for the crossing. The patriarch sold his sheep, the stepmother her tapestries, and the children the little trinkets they'd made for fun.

"As a result, some strange odysseys were being undertaken over the Mediterranean, our white sea, which would become tinged with the blood of future shipwrecks off the coast of Malta or Sicily.

"Carthago was full of desperate sailors and a great many small craft set sail from its shores. The numbers increased as the young people of this once magnificent city despaired of ever finding happiness.

"Most of the crew were recruited from the Libyan coast, on the Gulf of Sirte or in Tripoli, and there were many black Africans among them. The crossing was pleasant. It lasted three weeks. By the end, we were literally dying of hunger and thirst. I would have been tempted to eat one of my young companions if I hadn't retained a little of that sensitivity instilled in me by the education my grandmother, Lalla Fatima, gave me. She spent her nights telling me exciting stories of ogres who devoured reckless children. The idea had revolted me and I couldn't bring myself to draw lots, as suggested by Robinson, a fellow who still had some physical strength, but who was clearly losing his mind.

"'The person who draws the short straw can eat that child over there.' Robinson was serious. He looked first at me, then the child, and then came back to me, holding out his hand so that I could pick a piece of straw.

"'I'm not hungry, but thanks all the same,' I said, staring at the poor kid who was drying out under the sun, like a flower between the pages of a book.

"Often when the sea was flat, it shimmered with silvery glints that blinded me. When it grew choppier, it cast up bright gems that hypnotized the children into falling asleep, lulled by the regular sound of the bow slicing through the waves.

"In the evenings, the boat's occupants watched the white foam left behind by the boat and the phosphorescence within it, little lights that winked on and off, then flickered out."

III

WE WEATHERED STORMS for several nights. The sea swelled, striking fear into our hearts, and we had to cling on for fear of falling overboard. Having a poetic soul, I watched the celestial fire silently spilling onto the black water at regular intervals. When I eventually fell asleep, my eyes were filled with those flashes of frozen electricity that made my eyelids flutter open like an epileptic's and left me with a numb tongue and a head full of cotton wool. Then we ran out of fuel and the engine died, so we drifted.

For a long time, we made no headway on the oily surface, barely borne along by the currents. This lasted an eternity while the terrible heat hammered out its judgement on the weakest among us, the children and women who were barely conscious. We covered our heads with shirts, blankets and a fishing jacket found in the bottom of the small boat. We rationed the water and there wasn't enough food to go round. Sometimes, a flying fish fell into the boat and we devoured it raw, without the slightest sense of revulsion.

Finally, in the scorching heat of the sun, we ran aground on the island of Gozo, where we were helped by the UNHCR's dedicated teams. They nursed us back to health and gave us shelter in a camp. They questioned us for days, trying to establish who came from where, so that they would know where to send everyone back to. Naturally, no one told them anything, because we'd already all burnt our passports. In Carthago, we were called

39

the Harragas—"those who burn"—refugees who set fire to their identity papers. This colourful language appealed to me, Sinbad, a man who'd got himself into this unholy mess through his own stupid fault.

The refugee camp looked promising. It had every modern convenience you could wish for. Barbed wire protected the survivors from the locals, who wanted to string them up, and watchtowers guarded them as they slept peacefully. Soldiers armed by the UN, as in Rwanda, kept a close eye on this starving multitude which was in danger of overrunning Europe. My companions and I were lodged comfortably in metal shacks which could hold around thirty beds, with space to spare.

We were allowed to wander where we liked among those huge shelters, and even fearlessly go up to the barbed-wire fences, while waiting for our bowl of food.

We sometimes ran short of water and had to ration it, but that just meant that we didn't take showers. It was no worse than being at sea.

In line with UN standards, the food was good. Although completely tasteless, it provided the necessary calories to keep an organism going. The living conditions were acceptable.

You had free board and lodging for months before being sent home, if you didn't die of despair first.

"But it's a concentration camp!" said Robinson, the same Robinson who had wanted to eat a child.

I had to spend what little money I had left to pay a refugee-smuggler to help me escape from this earthly paradise. After that, a Calabrian charitable organization transported us to Cetraro, where we were thrown into the tomato fields to work from morning till night in the hope of getting a residence permit. Carlo Moro was our generous benefactor, a man who boasted that he had sent fifteen ships filled with radioactive waste to the bottom of the sea. He was the owner, on paper at least, of an industrial-waste treatment plant. They had to make a living somehow, these Calabrians who had joined forces within a strange corporation, the 'Ndrangheta, the kind of consortium that is so widespread in Italy and has made the peninsula famous.

———

I WOULD HAVE LEFT my field of tomatoes and peppers and run as fast as my legs could carry me to the bus stop for Rome, if I had not, unfortunately, fallen in love with Vitalia, Carlo Moro's youngest daughter.

Vitalia was a voluptuous maiden with a quick tongue. When she saw me for the first time, she seemed a little shy. She lowered her eyelids and her long black lashes fluttered like little butterflies. That was all it took to entrance me and ensure that I willingly accepted the lousy conditions of my captivity. It begged the question whether Carlo Moro wasn't serving his innocent young daughter up to the men he'd enslaved.

I loved Vitalia and Vitalia loved life. She was like a plant or a wild animal. She danced in the wind and sea spray like a whirlwind of joy, trailing in her wake everything that brought life to Cetraro, a seaside resort frequented by European tourists who came to savour the delights of a radioactive sea.

I'd made friends with some of the other captives, foreigners working for nothing for men like Carlo Moro. The entire peninsula was living off the labour of thousands of illegal immigrants forced to pick tomatoes and peppers, press olives and harvest grapes; and be humiliated by men who treated them like animals.

Carlo Moro wasn't like that. He was a rogue with a heart of gold. His grandfather had come from Sicily and had instilled in him that sense of honour so famous on the island where Odysseus had narrowly avoided shipwreck. Those macho feelings had their drawbacks, which obviously caused me some concern, but it would be too boring to list them here.

It took a great deal of cunning to contrive a meeting with Vitalia once she had ordered me to do so with her long black lashes. The young woman was sweetly lascivious. Vitalia liked to undress in front of me and I was always torn between my burning desire and the chilling prospect of being caught in the act by Carlo Moro.

In the evening, quiet as a cat, she'd slip into my hut where I was relaxing with a book. When she undressed, revealing her full breasts, and I gazed at that spectacular body with its silken skin as she lightly caressed her hardened nipples with a slender hand, I couldn't help thinking of Caravaggio, sick with fever and all alone on a Tuscan beach. Then I would feel a terrible sadness that associated the marvels and raptures of the flesh with the black death celebrated by Homer. Vitalia drew closer and pressed her flat stomach against my face, arching her back so that I had to press my lips against her velvety skin. I followed the contours of her navel as my young mistress gave a low moan, quiet as the evening breeze over the beach, and I slipped my eager tongue inside her while, with my fingers, I spread the firm, round globes that completed the slope of her back. Then, in her deep, husky voice she sang a sort of song as my throat filled with the salty flood of the deep, and love, death, life and negated time spilled over my face, pinned between the thighs of a woman consumed by desire.

———

A LONE ON THE BEACH, I'd sketch Vitalia's body in the sand; it was often a long curve, like a child's drawing, or the simple lines executed by artists at the peak of their powers. Her long black hair followed the line of the waves caressing the shore; as the sea withdrew, it left behind mounds suggesting her stomach and breasts, the small of her back and her hips, rounded and full as the moon.

When she joined me in my hut, she would undress quickly and press her firm, lithe body against mine. These rapturous embraces would last all night. She would sometimes come and find me during the day and we'd hide behind a dune or a beach-house fence. Then she would remove my trousers or shorts and take me in her mouth, her wavy hair cascading over my thighs. She would devour me for long minutes while I enjoyed her, the sun, the silvery patches of light on her tanned skin, the surf, the breeze in the dry grass, and then I'd spill into her mouth and my semen flowed like lava over my stomach.

At other times, I'd pull her close and undress her like a deli-cate, silent doll. She'd let me lift up her flimsy dress and kiss her breasts. I'd spread her legs, she'd wriggle away like an eel, turn over laughing and arching her back, and I'd recapture her, cover her with my body, pushing myself between her buttocks without entering her, my face working its way up the nape of her neck to her fragrant mane of hair. An eternity passed as we remained locked together, entwined like mythical androgynes or those dyads created by the philosopher who remembered and reproduced his youthful passions as abstract images.

How old was Vitalia? She seemed very young sometimes during the day but, at night, she reached maturity, as if the moon in its fullness had endowed her with all the attributes of womanhood. Her age remained a mystery, though. She was no longer Carlo Moro's daughter, but Vitalia, princess by day, queen of the night, a goddess invented for me. She was siren and saint, virgin and whore, or even more nebulous, like a sacred image from the mind of a sailor in solitary confinement or trapped in the belly of the whale, who, to avoid dying of despair, fills his prison with paradisaical visions in which a woman fresh as a flower keeps him company.

The dream was shattered when Carlo Moro caught us making love. He attacked me, and a fierce fight ensued from which it was a miracle I escaped. I climbed out of the window to elude the jealous father, the way they do in films, and ran off into the night.

How many immigrants had met with a terrible fate for fondling a local man's daughter? They were accused of rape and strung up or stoned to death by the crowd—and with good reason, since the local press would always stand up for their homeland after it had been defiled by a foreigner. Even in Carthago, punitive actions were often taken against some boy caught with his hand up the skirt of a girl whose father, fiercely in favour of the death penalty, turned his neighbourhood against the enemy camp to such an extent that the descendants of the rival families would still be at war centuries later, even though they no longer knew the real reason for their enmity. Everyone has their Montagues and their Capulets. Or their Horatius and their Curiatii. When Horatia, Horatius's younger sister, came to meet her brother at the Porta Capena, she recognized the cloak of her betrothed, a Curiatius killed by Horatius, draped over her brother's shoulders. She loosed her hair and wept. His sister's laments aroused Horatius's wrath. He drew his sword and, stabbing the young woman in the heart, he upbraided her, crying, "Begone to your betrothed with your ill-timed love, since you have forgotten your brothers, both the dead and the living, and forgotten your country."

And he added, "So perish every Roman woman who mourns a foe!"

After killing three Curiatii, the valiant Horatius murdered his own sister, Horatia.

Terrible Horatius should have been executed for this crime. He appealed to the people who pardoned him, still exhilarated by his victories over the Curiatii. From that time on, it was the right of any Roman citizen, faced with the threat of death or exile, to be judged by the populace, if he so desired. This custom came in very handy and allowed many murderers to escape punishment for their heinous crimes.

I was on the beach, hidden behind some lentisk trees, when I heard the sound of cascading water. The noise speeded up as though someone had turned on a tap in the dry grass. I dropped Livy and his Roman histories, stood up and, burning with curiosity, headed for the musical waters. Behind a small shrub squatted a woman with her skirt hiked up over her shapely legs, and white lace panties around her ankles. When she saw me, Sinbad, looking like a noble savage from some storybook or an Odysseus washed up on the shores of Phaeacia, she gave a cry of surprise and attempted to stand up. Naturally she fell over backwards and the wet earth soiled her white panties. I apologized and held out my hand to the young woman, pretending to look away to spare her blushes. She scrambled to her feet, pulled her skirt down over her thighs, and threw the flimsy panties into the bushes.

"I couldn't hold it in any longer," she said guilelessly.

She spoke in French with a slight southern accent and a hint of Italian musicality. It was delightful. My first thought was that I, Sinbad, who had been living on this beach to escape the clutches of Carlo Moro, certainly hadn't expected to meet a woman who cared so little about her modesty in such compromising circumstances. Giovanna had the bold soul of a Man Friday. I was her Man Saturday. She grabbed my hand and led me away, as Nausicaa had once done with her Odysseus.

———

G IOVANNA LIVED IN ROME and worked at the famous Villa Medici, where she assisted its no less famous director, Corneille Paduzzi di Balto, a writer, producer and painter in his spare time; a painter of little girls. He'd sketched Giovanna at the age of twelve, lying languidly on a sofa, her short blue skirt pulled up over her thighs and her short-sleeved blouse open over her barely developed breasts. The picture was now in the collection of the famous Henri-François Donadieu and could be seen in a well-known gallery in Venice. Giovanna told everyone that Paduzzi di Balto's pencil had barely touched her and that he hadn't defiled her youthful beauty. If he had, she would never have continued to work for the *direttore*.

In private, when she pressed her firm, lithe body against mine, it was another story: it wasn't just his pencil that the *famoso direttore* had used on the young Giovanna.

She was proud of sacrificing her innocence to her Pygmalion's masterful artistry. Paduzzi di Balto was now very old, so he hardly ever left his ground-floor apartment in the Villa Medici; he no longer had enough strength to paint his small-scale models. He could no longer pin butterflies to his canvases, like the famous writer whose name he'd now forgotten; he languished and waited for death by his window overlooking the gardens of the Renaissance residence, where tall umbrella pines stood silhouetted against the Roman sky. If he happened to walk past one of those water nymphs, he would give chase, but he never caught one.

When I arrived at the Villa, the *maestro* was already a mere shadow of his former self. He had to be kept away from these Lolitas—not because they were in any particular danger from the poor *direttore*, but because he might embark on a headlong chase through thickets and over lawns, clambering over old stones and through murderous brambles, in hot pursuit of the young objects of his fantasies without any care for his own safety. If he were to fall, this ninety-year-old Solomon ran the risk of ending up with limbs dislocated like a puppet's and dying in the very place he had sinned, or almost. So the staff, who were all members of the same Abruzzi family who, generation after generation, had been appointed to imaginary posts in the noble academy, donned kid gloves to handle the old fool, as they called him.

Giovanna had been his last victim and the experience had left her with the type of nervous complications suffered by those who have come into contact too early with the harsh realities of art. She had eaten of the fruit while it was still unripe and was having to strain to pass the stone. Her behaviour could be very strange. She was cheerful and captivating one minute, and so melancholy and depressed the next that you had to hide sharp or pointed objects from her, keep her away from windows and bind her wrists to stop her trying to cut them. Weeks would also go by when she was perfectly stable, healthy in body and mind. Then suddenly she would have a complete emotional and physical meltdown. I couldn't get over her inventiveness and her remarkable flexibility in bed. At those times, she was a whispering, screaming ball of passion. Fortunately, we lived in one of the pavilions at the far end of the garden, beside the Orange Tree Garden, where the ghosts of former residents gathered and chatted about Villa affairs.

These ghosts were the damned souls of earlier lodgers, second-rate artists who'd been exiled from France to the sinister city of Rome. The poor souls had departed this life in the Villa in the nineteenth century and were still roaming their Golgotha. The only ones to escape were Berlioz, who went on to compose and orchestrate the huge Witches' Sabbath of his *Symphonie Fantastique*, a *danse macabre* inspired by the Villa and Rome, and Debussy, who'd survived academic failure to be the famous composer of endangered, moonlit music. I also wondered if the man who composed *Carmen* wouldn't come to haunt the Orange Tree

Garden, since he never recovered from his stay in this hellhole and died on his return to Paris, although not before he'd had time to present the world with his terrifying opera created from lies, borrowings from Spanish music and lecherous practices taught him by the whores of Rome.

IV

FROM MY WINDOW, I could see the umbrella pines. The sky over the greys of Rome. The countless towns overlapping each other along the Tiber, between the seven hills. And Carthago, in the distance, swallowed up by memory and terrible massacres, while death did the rounds like a popular rumour. I heard the noise of boots, the clatter of weapons, the yells. I thought about my father. My mother died when I was seven, my magic number, so I'd been raised by that old woman, Lalla Fatima, who told me stories about horrible legends, awful tales about a Sleeper and his dog, about seven avengers who would wake at the end of time. I lived in fear of witnessing the arrival of that day. Of course, it never came or, rather, almost never, since you're here now with your dog.

My father had disappeared like Romulus, abducted by the gods of the time: the henchmen employed by the reign of terror that started in Carthago after the Romans left. Or the French. I was losing track of invasions and mixing up periods. The sanctuary-town of Carthago was no help in sorting out my memories. The town embodied the history of a sunken civilization. Even its name should have disappeared without trace after the havoc wreaked by the Romans, its soil blighted by fire and salt to prevent rebirth.

And yet it had risen again from its ashes, gathering up its bloody rags and soaring towards a glorious sky, before tumbling back into enslavement. That was another story totally irrelevant to the life of a modern man born with the invention of the moon and colour TV. I didn't care a jot about History with a capital "H", that bloodthirsty goddess who had slyly got her hooks into me in the form of a civil war—the terrible plague that had befallen this new Thebes, where every son had become a mighty Oedipus, murdering his father and sleeping with his mother between sticky sheets. Yes, Carthago had hatched new fires that were even more destructive than the ones lit by the ragtag Roman soldiers.

So I was a fearful, unambitious child, who understood nothing of the world around him. I was ill-prepared for the life I was going to lead as an adult once I'd completely frittered away the fortune I'd inherited from my father, once I'd left to travel the paths of the world, driven by need. I found myself in Rome, thrown into the She-Wolf's den by one of those tricks played by history. Rome had burnt Carthago to the ground, holding it up to public ridicule and forbidding the construction of new ramparts to replace the old ones. Rome, the enemy of Africa, and yet no less African, noisy, dusty and drowsy under a sun that encouraged flies and ancient acts of violence.

———

P EOPLE DON'T LIKE travelling and that's a fact. Or else they're tourists. Rome was overflowing with them. You should have seen them in the Piazza di Spagna, forming a dense mass around Bernini's boat fountain, like flies on fresh dung or a decaying carcass, the gamy meat of an outdated concept: art. Art was finished now; people kissed relics en masse but threw shit at artists, who were allowed to die like fish out of water, suffocating with their gills gaping open. No witnesses, no pilgrims wandering into the void to sniff at the artists' arses, just a few curious onlookers, watching the beached creatures' convulsions and applauding as if they were at the circus. In fact, if you went out into the desolate square early in the morning, you could see that Bernini's fountain wasn't half bad—it was even rather beautiful, set against the backdrop of the staircase leading up to the church of Trinità dei Monti. It had style, that gallant, lonely boat sailing towards a cascade of steps, en route to glory, preparing to climb its Calvary, hailed by Keats. But, sadly, the church was sheathed, Roman-style, in a giant advertisement, like some promotional condom. What an eyesore! And those Hominids in shorts, with their fat, slovenly, rowdy, sanctimonious females who were certainly not a pretty sight with all that flabby flesh, that composition of stretch marks, varicose veins and a hundredweight of faecal matter. Since the death of the Immobile Pope, the city was always packed, overrun by the barbarian hordes who were in danger of blocking up the sewers and causing a shitty *acqua alta*. The world was going to the dogs, particularly if no one put a stop to this influx. Adventures were out of the question now: there were no more empty spaces, no more wildernesses.

I thought back to ancient times when the first navigators, like my distant ancestor, the Sinbad of legend, sailed the Indian Ocean, but they never encountered these freaks in shorts, their photographic muzzles crowned by baseball caps. In those blessed, long-forgotten times, you could still die alone on a deserted beach like Caravaggio.

Finding a desolate shore now was unlikely. Lost in memories, I watched the ghosts of those who had inhabited my childhood. My father would take me fishing on the beaches of Carthago at a time when those beaches allowed such magical escapades. It was before the war that cast a dark glow over my youth. There were such depths to the night under the Milky Way: that long spermatic tail fertilizing thousands of stars, which squirmed in the dark like maggots.

I walked to Piazza Navona to take my mind off things. Here, as well, clouds of horseflies twitched over the magnificent circus and around the Fountain of the Four Rivers: Bernini facing off against Borromini, then taking fright. The place was submerged under the reds, yellows and greens of the umbrellas used to guide the oxen traipsing past like a strange species of centipede. Various painters had set up their ridiculous easels to sketch the stuck-up American cows, attracted by the smell of death, who thought Rome *so romantic*. The Immobile Pope had just joined the Polish angels and was hanging over the city like the stench of decomposition, intensified by the mingling sweat of millions of holidaymakers gathered here in pursuit of eternity.

"Who are you then?"

"Just a tourist… like all the rest."

Not like the rest. I stayed here to drink this town to the dregs and die here, unable to pull myself free. Rome and Italy were buried under the weight of scandal, suffocated by madmen who'd been looting them for a century. Men like Carlo Moro were legion and they worked hard to retain power. They had even created their own Golem, a kind of jester, a Milanese industrialist, spawned by the P4 secret lodge, who had grown up in troubled times and who owed his great wealth to his mafia connections. The Golem had monopolized the media and, now, the pale windows of TV screens reflected his gargoyle of a face between adverts. Pandering to the population's baser instincts, the man had brought Ancient Roman games into line with modern tastes and now, instead of Christians providing the entertainment, a collection of poor sods paraded their private lives before millions of spectators. In between bloody sparring matches, young ladies, who were half-naked and preferably blonde, strutted around and commented on these pitiful confessions in shocked, strident tones. No one had ever seen such a mind-numbing initiative. Watching Italian television was like abandoning all hope, the way Dante had before the gates of his Inferno.

The Golem was like a Roman emperor: old Tiberius, for example. He possessed all the same attributes.

And yet I was enjoying myself at the Villa Medici. Giovanna had put me in the pavilion of that runaway writer whose name was no longer spoken on pain of excommunication (St Peter's was just a stone's throw away, after all). The hack had left behind all his things, among them his books and an unfinished manuscript: *The New Voyages of Sinbad*, which described the famous sailor's new adventures. It was a strange novel, in which Sinbad's adventures were all carnal. To my utmost delight, the sailor kept moving on from one woman to the next, so I didn't put down the book until I'd finished it. It felt odd to meet yourself in a novel, to see your double doing things in your place and behaving like a scoundrel. But wasn't that what literature was for: to hold up a vulgar mirror to our lives? That's why writers were hated by their contemporaries, and I'm talking about real writers here. For example, in Carthago we're very proud to number some scholarly torturers among our ranks. We mustn't mistake the pen for the red-hot iron, or the sacred fire for the Electric Fairy; or confuse bathing in the fountain of youth, which is so vital for art, with wallowing in a bathtub of sorrowful memories. I for one have never mixed them up. I know a few writers who advertise their own worth. They are well-liked, and people kiss their arses in Europe. They are our high priests of literature. Our policemen of prose. Our incendiary cardinals. Our inquisitors. Those quill-pushers are celebrated throughout the world for their warlike exploits and their literary triviality. Something is rotten in the literary kingdom of Carthago. Let's move swiftly on. I've never liked the scum who sit scribbling in their rooms and call that travelling. I'm the priest of open spaces, I'm the cloud with its trousers on fire. Live fast, go to the ends of the earth, love to the utmost: that's my manifesto.

So I felt a little cooped up in that magnificent mansion. I was pining for my darling Vitalia. And yet, the Villa Medici was divided into two separate, and totally different, areas. Your idea of self dictated where you lived. The residents called the group of houses at the far end of the Villa Medici's grounds *Sarcelles*; while the rest, the delightful studios or *studioli*, were named *Neuilly*, showing the wicked sense of irony that prevailed in this place, given that the real Sarcelles is a poverty-stricken suburb of Paris. I loved this part of the garden; I loved the absence of luxury and ostentation in those graceless houses which were clearly a late addition. Anyway, our Sarcelles was not really Sarcelles, because you only had to push open a gate to find yourself in Via Veneto or at Porta Pinciana, which is one of the wealthiest districts in Rome, where whores still hang around the streets as they did in the time of Tennessee Williams.

In 1948, Tennessee Williams discovered Rome. The youthful playwright, whose *A Streetcar Named Desire* had just been a massive success, walked along the Via Veneto in search of young boys. He disappeared down the paths of the Villa Borghese gardens. It makes me smile to think that, some sixty years apart, we walked along the same side streets. I haven't yet acquired as much of a taste for boys as him, so it's probably better to play down this amusing coincidence.

Anyway, everyone when in Rome has rushed down the Via Veneto, the famous avenue from *La Dolce Vita*, which was, and continues to be, the Romans' Champs-Élysées. It would be hard to imagine an uglier avenue, but it seems to have appealed to our playwright desperate for sensual experience:

"As for prostitution, that is really the world's oldest profession in all Mediterranean countries with the possible exception of Spain. It is due largely to their physical beauty and to their warmth of blood, their natural eroticism. In Rome you rarely see a young man who does not have a slight erection. Often they walk along the Veneto with hand in pocket, caressing their genitals quite unconsciously, and this regardless of whether or not they are hustling or cruising. They are raised without any of our puritanical reserves about sex."

The Romans don't tend to play with themselves in the street nowadays. As for the prostitutes, I've glimpsed a few around the Villa in the evening, waiting for clients.

———

" THE RIGHT WAY to travel is not knowing anyone in the places you're visiting, or hardly anyone; you should not have any letters of recommendation to hand over, or any meetings to keep; you should have no appointments with anyone but yourself, so that you can see the things—in a region, in a town—that you wanted to see at your leisure, although, speaking purely for myself, there are usually not many. Of course, meeting people can also reveal a great deal about what we generally call *the spirit of a place*; but that is not so much in evidence as before and it is better, in any case, to admire this spirit in things instead. Thirty years ago, I travelled with a great deal of freedom and a great deal of pleasure; now, my endless meetings and commitments mean that I travel with very little freedom, and not so much pleasure.

"The list of things I want to see, prepared before my departure or imagined for so long, always ends up being cut outrageously short or drastically changed by my obligations, which always seem to multiply unexpectedly. This is already happening during my short stay in Madrid. Fortunately, I've been here before."

Leonardo Sciascia vindicated my solitude. I read his *Spanish Moments*, shut away in my room: a vast chamber with a mezzanine and a coffered ceiling which was almost twenty feet high. I kept the room dimly lit to make reading easier.

Outside, Rome is baking at the beginning of May, or June, or July. I have no idea which month it is. Only my reading keeps me here at the Villa Medici, and the weather doesn't matter. I remain alone in my room, devouring books.

I go out at nightfall when the heat is less unbearable, the light not so harsh and the streets not so crowded.

Then I explore the darkened, dazzling alleys of the town. A strange bluish, peaceful light engulfs the ochre stone. I walk alone across the Corso, along the Piazza Colonna, and turn into the Piazza della Rotonda.

The first time, in broad daylight, it was like a vision.

The building had ripped through the web of time: the spacecraft, sent by an extra-terrestrial civilization, had landed on the town, tearing open the houses and narrow streets. It was the loveliest ancient ruin I'd ever been lucky enough to see, as well as the most frightening. It was a dark mouth beneath the sky and I thought it had a barbaric beauty. It exuded a feeling of sacredness; but not a scalloped baroque sacredness which was timeworn and harmless. Not a bit of it. This witness to a most violent past flattened the surrounding district the way a rampaging elephant crushes the soldiers at its feet. The tragic monument of the Pantheon spewed out the blood of holocausts.

Opposite, on the Piazza della Rotonda, the fountain by Giacomo Della Porta stands tall at the centre of its basin. The light pulses in the electric water and climbs up to attack the grotesque water-spouts. Under the grimacing gods, the corners are teeming with cockroaches. They are a brilliant glossy black. For a moment I think with delight of the tourists dipping their hands into the water to cool themselves. These creatures aren't out of keeping with this place. They are well suited to the Pantheon as rebuilt by Hadrian. They nest in the folds of the malevolent mind who presided over the reconstruction of this place of worship. The Christians, then the Muslims, were kind-hearted in comparison;

no one ever smelled the blood of sacrifices within a church or the courtyard of a mosque. It's much better like this, thinks the modern fool: ancient practices like being mauled to death by wild animals or dispatched by a priest's sword in front of the Pantheon are a thing of the past, but what was banished from the ancient temple now roams the streets. They burn down the houses and the people who live in them; they mow down the world's children and women by bombing the towns: they no longer hold sacrifices, of course, but they reduce men to dust and ashes instead. It's cleaner, more dispassionate, less visible.

Beside the murmuring basin, where the black armies crawled, I remembered the epic of Hannibal.

Carthago had seized control of all Phoenician trading posts in the West as a means of opposing Greek colonization.

Carthago...

Picture a city in the sea, linked to the African continent by a spit of land. A cove wound about by ships.

A stroll through Cadiz is enough to give you an idea of that city engulfed by history.

A former Carthaginian trading post, Cadiz, the Gades of Hamilcar Barca, Hannibal's father, is still similar in spirit to its African cousin. This town stretches out into the sea and is linked to the mainland by a peninsula, as I was to see for myself one day when I had visited both cities.

After a terrible, deeply upsetting visit to Granada, I stayed in Cadiz for several weeks, not without making a detour to Seville, where the Alcazar gardens and the cherry trees in bloom look so beautiful in the shifting light of March, at the very start of spring: the town is covered in a jasmine-scented cloud, and the streets around the Giralda, the old Moorish quarter, the Juderia, the Jewish ghetto, and the magical patios silently unfold in the sunshine, like penitents in a procession during the *semana santa*...

It was at Megara, a suburb of Carthage, in the gardens of the Alcazar...

SALIM BACHI

I loved *Salammbô*, the book that set me dreaming during my adolescence in Carthago. I'd discovered it in a bookshop beneath a pile of books. The shop-soiled copy didn't look like a good read for a young man who was still lured by garish illustrations and eye-catching images, none of which adorned its cover. It took me quite a while to read the first sentence of the novel, reluctantly, as if already bored in advance.

It was at Megara, a suburb of Carthage, in the gardens of Hamilcar.

Strolling along the ramparts of Cadiz is enough to plunge visitors into the dream of a city destroyed by the fury of men. Reading *Salammbô* is enough to make anyone fall under the spell of an Orient that shared very little in common with my own private Carthago. It shimmered with an unfamiliar light. It contained profound rapture, frightening destruction. I became a Carthaginian, a Greek merchant, a sacred whore who kissed a serpent and loved it like a man or woman, or something even stranger: I very soon became convinced that love is a mystery worshipped by the ancient religions. I began to seek out women's favours even more fervently, in the anticipation that I'd discover hidden treasure there, a promise of infinite knowledge and pleasure.

V

I was missing vitalia, and this brought on a somewhat melancholy mood which made me view Rome in a jaundiced light. I kept looking for her in the streets of the Eternal City. I rushed down the Via Veneto thinking of her sweet face. I visited the Barberini Museum and came to a halt, almost floating on air, before *La Fornarina* by Raphael, the Renaissance painter whom I revered as much as Giotto and Fra Angelico.

La Fornarina deserves to be better known than the *Mona Lisa*. The bakeress was the painter's mistress, who allegedly loved him to death. I had almost suffered the same fate between Vitalia's arms and thighs. She dealt with me the way a laundress beats her washing, then thoroughly wrings it dry.

Vitalia, La Fornarina, both brunettes with haunting eyes. A finger rests on the breast of one woman, whose large open eyes declare their desire for the visitor or casual lover. I understood Raphael: I fell in love with the woman in the painting. I continually mistook her for my one true Vitalia, my amazing magic lamp. All I had to do was rub her and she let out a demon. That lascivious genie granted all my wishes; he fulfilled my wildest desires, and my desires were endless, as were those of the Vatican's painter when he brought his French stick to the oven or gave it to the young brunette with shining eyes so that she could knead it with hands as dainty as a Madonna's, her small, round breasts like little brioches.

I explored Vitalia's body like a cartographer mapping an unknown land, constantly measuring the distances covered, drawing up increasingly detailed reports.

I knew every promontory, every valley and every hill in this realm of pleasures and exotic fragrances. She rarely wore perfume and never wore make-up, except for lining her lashes with kohl, which made her dark gazelle eyes seem even larger. She oozed a delicate, heavy liquor. Her skin smelled of jasmine in the morning and amber at night. Her parted thighs opened into a welcoming darkness redolent of the lingering scent of damp grass.

With my probing nose between her buttocks, I again sailed across the sea buffeted by storms and tempests, I burned under the throbbing sun, my lungs filled with sea spray and iodine, my eyes with flashes of frozen electricity. When I penetrated her, I became a ship with a conquering stern, a proud prow parting the foam. The sea beneath my body moaned and writhed, withdrew and pulled me close, then moaned again, as tireless as the tide.

Such ecstasy could have sent me to the grave too, if the hateful Carlo Moro had not put an end to our love which, with the help of absence, now acquired a mystical edge. The lack of Vitalia, of her body driven wild with desire and burning hot as lava, created a love as infinite as the sky.

Walking through the gardens of the Villa Borghese, I saw her behind every tree, every copse, as if this were some enchantment described by Ovid, in which the plants and flowers were captive girls transformed by a god or jealous goddess as a punishment: she was both the girl laughing as she kissed her fiancé and the old lady out walking with her granddaughter; she was the gently trodden grass, the dirt track in the rain, the October air inhaled as my stay in Rome was drawing to a close. Vitalia filled me with sap like spring, dried me out like August, and drained my strength like a languid autumn. I became the leaf in the wind that falls uncaring from a loveless tree.

It was as I was walking along the Corso, lost in my memories, that I heard a shout:

"Sinbad! Sinbad! My friend!"

I turned and saw a man crouching in front of a church, clapping his hands to attract my attention. He was tall and black.

"Robinson! What are you doing here?"

Robinson had a pavement shop. He was selling posters of Bob Dylan, Bob Marley, Janis Joplin and Mussolini. In Rome, you could obtain images of Il Duce quite freely. You have to remember that Rome was an open-minded city; a city where the Guide's granddaughter was pursuing an honourable career in politics by invoking her illustrious grandfather's name.

"Robinson, what are you doing selling that…"

I pointed to the dictator's blunt chin.

"My dear Sinbad, I have to make a living. The Romans love their history. They're proud of it… Not like we Africans."

"Still, Robinson, not him…"

"I've got some portraits of Bokassa, but no one knows who he is here. We only have small-time tyrants. Who's heard of Boumediene, for example?"

"No one, you're right."

"Those crooks aren't capable of hassling anyone other than their own people. Total losers."

"But, all the same, you are black and that bastard didn't like darkies!"

"No one likes anyone," said Robinson, as though stating an eternal truth. "Except you, dear Sinbad. You're a good man, and an innocent one. A noble man, as we say in Senegal. You ought to hate me. My grandfather was in the Senegalese infantry corps. He must have killed some of your lot during the events in Sétif and Guelma in 1945."

"No one remembers the eighth of May."

"I remember everything, Sinbad. And I know that Lazio's supporters love Mussolini and let me work in peace when they see I respect their great man. They don't hunt me like a dog through the streets of the *Città*."

I was struck dumb by this notion of the survival of the weakest. The Senegalese was making good sense, no doubt about it.

"Before you go, Sinbad, take this."

Robinson held out an amulet.

"It will bring you luck. You'll see her again, don't worry. She's waiting for you."

"I'll see who again?"

"Vitalia, Sinbad, Vitalia!"

———

I DIDN'T GET MUCH SLEEP the night after I'd bumped into Robinson. My back was aching when I got up. As I didn't fancy breakfasting with the residents at the Villa, I went for a stroll in the direction of the Piazza del Popolo. I set out along the Via del Babuino as far as the vast round, or oval, square with its twin churches. Behind me was the steep climb towards the Pincio and the gardens where young couples fool around in broad daylight. I thought about Vitalia, and a little about Robinson crouching behind his posters, his African trinkets, and his Lazio supporters.

In front of me, beyond the square, was the deeply embanked Tiber, inaudible and invisible. I sat on the stairs leading down to the riverside. Mingled scents of flowers and urine. The riverbanks were deserted. The river flowed past, majestic, emerald green, alone, like a long prison sentence under the sky. People don't tend to stroll by the Tiber the way they walk beside the Seine. The Romans are wary of their river. Not that long ago, it had been infested with mosquitoes, malaria-carriers.

I was still reading *Spanish Moments*, far from the city's noise, on the steps down to the embankment. It was pleasant in the shade, the warm air filling my shirt, blowing gently through the trees. I listened to the rustling of the leaves. A father and his two children sat down beside me, even though the Tiber was deserted for several hundred yards. A man can never be alone, especially if he's comfortable somewhere.

I stood up, walked back across the Piazza del Popolo and climbed the steps up to the Pincio. The walk to the Villa Medici is one of the most beautiful in Rome. The road between the trees overlooked the town and its terraces. Under the garlands of wisteria, I felt a huge surge of renewed life. The scorching sun fell on me between the leaves and the burning patches on my skin flowed like clear water as time passed and the walk seemed to last for ever.

There, between the carob trees, on the road to the Trinità dei Monti, I decided to visit Florence. Why Florence? I didn't know. I had dreamt about the city of Dante and Brunelleschi since I was a child. I went back to my room, packed my case and ordered a taxi for Termini station. I waited a long time for the train, as is customary in Rome where nothing happens quickly. I was used to that. I'd spent years waiting when I was living in Carthago, the city of unfulfilled desires. Finally, the train came and, two hours later, I was walking through the streets of the stone city which was shrouded in mist. A beggar woman was imploring the pavement for help. It was growing dark. The Palazzo Vecchio was lit up. Pale lights. Cold lights. The beggar woman was dying on the frozen cobblestones of Florence. Another of those creatures from Albania, trafficked by mercenaries who had then abandoned her to her fate.

As the statues looked on: Perseus holding Medusa's head at arm's length; David with drawn sword, his eyes rebellious beneath an elegant headdress.

The impassive gaze of the gods.
Hotel Alighieri.

I climbed the rickety staircase up to my room. I emptied my pockets onto the bed. Not much there. No money. No honey. I'd have to go out begging. I was an ancient god. Was I going to lose my sight? Be led by my daughter from place to place to recount the woes of the man greedy for knowledge who murdered his father and slept with his mother? There are times when I was afraid of failing, like the poor beggar woman who looked so much like me she could have been my sister. Shipwrecked creatures held a mirror up to my life, reflecting my destiny like the fate of the Porter from the legend that saw me born into another story, among the pages of an old manuscript found in a Cairo market at the end of the nineteenth century, and translated by strange adventurers who knew Arabic and haggled over the treasures of the Orient.

Did anyone still know what the *Arabian Nights* was? People didn't read any more. They watched the Golem's television, which now reached across the whole wide world, while cargoes of slaves died: the poor sods drowned at sea or perished by the executioner's machete while the West had fun. But I didn't feel any hatred. I walked quietly and sensibly through the city of rebirth, where Giotto had executed his first shaft of light.

The cobblestones were shining like worms.

I could still see.

Phew.

A bar.

Men and women lounging on long ottomans. Lounging in the smoke. In a room filled with long, smoky ottomans. Men. And women. In the late-night heat of this enclosed place.

Inferno!

64

"Virgilio! Virgilio! *Per cortesia, una birra!*"

Virgilio pulled a beer.

The whisper of the lager.

"The same, please."

Virgilio doesn't understand.

Damned language!

An enquiring glance from Virgilio.

"Virgilio! *Una birra!*"

A young woman has just spoken to the barman. He put a beer mug in front of me. I glanced at my good Samaritan. She nodded to me. I nodded back and moved closer to her.

"You speak..."

"Stendhal is my favourite author."

He was mine too. Or that's what I said.

"Virgilio, that's an odd name."

"It's very old. My name is Beatrice."

I apologized that I couldn't buy her a drink. As Rimbaud said, I'd gone off with my hands in my coat pockets and my overcoat was becoming ideal. Giovanna hadn't had time to give me any money. I'd run off without seeing her; I didn't want to be saddled with questions, promises or tears.

Beatrice allowed me to walk back with her. We left Virgilio's cave, just a few yards from the Santa Croce church where Michelangelo lies until Judgement Day. His tomb, near the entrance, faced the Duomo, the first treasure that the sculptor wanted to see when he rose with the dead on the Day of Resurrection.

Outside, a cool mist hung above the cobblestones. Beatrice light-heartedly talked about Stendhal, literature and Renaissance Florence. She followed me back to my hotel room. I sensed that she would have followed me to the ends of the earth if I'd wanted, but I didn't put it to the test, in case she formed too strong an attachment. I refused to live beyond my means, while my mind wandered through the maze of narrow cobbled streets, between the mansions whose thick façades prevented me from appreciating the true charm of exquisite chambers where bronze boys frolicked, a catapult hanging from their fine-boned hands. Beatrice, like every other proud and poetic Laura, required her lovers to provide a wealth of poetry that I no longer possessed. My lost boyhood in Carthago, that vile town, had denied me most of the delights found only in a carefree childhood. I'd experienced war and its horrors. My own body had felt the impact of an explosion which destroyed my town and spread desolation along its shores.

Beatrice was also a child, but without the excuse of youth like Vitalia, whom I rediscovered in Beatrice's body, although the latter was blonde, and smelled of fire and iron while Vitalia wore the fragrance of dawning summer. I felt just as happy loving her, though. I lost myself in the same way between her legs, which were as long as the Arno snaking its way through Tuscany. When she straddled my stomach, she was like the Ponte Vecchio over the river bed.

Her bellybutton and her breasts, like treasures unfolding before the eyes of an idle stroller, formed a picture or fresco similar to those adorning the walls of convents and churches, which eternal-ized the glory of the city where I liked to lose myself. Beatrice had Beauty's throat of marble, which bruised and chilled her lover's mouth. Perplexed by so much violence, splattered with gold, I burned in my turn like the lamp in the Qur'an, that sacred flame whose light illuminated the world. Beneath my mistress's ardent body, flooded by her desire, made fertile by the ebb and flow of silt-laden waters, I was consumed like the olive wood in the Qur'an, in Beatrice's flesh, a poem become river.

———

B EATRICE WAS TWELVE when she experienced love for the first time. The man was a *poète maudit* whose every endeavour ended in failure. All that he had to show for himself were his new poems and a short, pointless life which, for all that, was to influence generations of men to come. What was his name? Beatrice refused to tell me. Perhaps he was dead, and his face was fading from collective memory after being captured by one of those painters who were to make Florence famous. He had been born too late: Giotto had already departed this world.

I didn't give a damn about Dante; I travelled inside Beatrice like a pilgrim bracing himself on his staff. I slipped inside her like a trout or a blessed fish, rubbing my scales over her smooth skin, insinuating myself like the serpent in the lovers' Eden. We were the whole world, I was the eternal Adam and she was the primordial Eve. I kissed her Madonna's hands the way I'd once kissed the face of La Donna Velata, Raphael's lascivious lover, arrayed like a saint, which made her even more desirable. But is loving convent virgins the only way to experience this sweet turmoil? Nothing is less certain, even if the modern alternative is not so appealing: loving only women the same age as you means turning your back on most kinds of love. Beatrice was ageless. She had sprung from those far-off centuries when all women looked like adolescents; when all the prostitutes in Florence inspired an imprudent Lippi or an austere Botticelli.

On the occasions that I recalled Florence, it was Beatrice's face I saw, the woman's face, instead of the city which took on finely nuanced colours as the days went by. The uneven, rectangular cobblestones regained their former sheen. The city woke forever under Beatrice's inquisitive gaze, which was filled with surprise at the renewed wonder shown by a corsair at the prow of his galliot on a rising, rebellious tide. The city's laughter filled my ears and merged with the lapping of the river that flowed past, telling us that Time made no difference because, although we might be breathing and walking now, sooner or later we'd have to give up our place and be swaddled in a shroud and cast into oblivion. The only things that remained eternally alive were La Donna Velata's smile, in which our dreams entwined; Fra Angelico's winged angels glimpsed fleetingly on the first floor of the San Marco Convent, intimate and hushed as a shell; or the crotch of a trollop burning with youthful passion and the play of light on her face as rendered by the greatest painters. Florence was like Ali Baba's cave. An unpretentious-looking palace, holed up behind high walls, yet containing all the relics of the world, the hard work of artists who had died over five centuries ago; their souls lived on in the walls and the lanes near the Arno, through which you had to stoop, and where you could easily imagine that the shops and gloomy studios were caves in which the images of a civilization had been created. It was weird and wonderful to follow in the footsteps of those guardians of memory. It was impossible to imagine a better quest. Verrocchio's impish David continued on his way alongside Perseus who, still a boy, was brandishing a severed head.

As the days passed, my mood grew darker. My outings with Beatrice depressed me. The city's charms began to pall. My thoughts returned to Vitalia, who kept coming back like rheumatic fever to the heart, a fatal condition afflicting me every morning on waking. I wished for her skin, soft as a peach, her breath like a jasmine flower intoxicated by the star over the Giralda. I shall remember those nights I spent in Seville until the end of time, long after I've forgotten my stay in Italy. I went there to cure an illness, when I was bone-tired, already mature and weary of so many adventures. I wasn't just running away from the dramas of a man without family or friends, who travelled from port to port, carried along by desire, exiled from perpetual exile.

Beatrice noticed and didn't put up a fight or try to hold me back. It wouldn't have done any good. She let me disappear down the Arno, my thoughts in turmoil, sailing to my misfortune down all the rivers of the wide world.

In Carthago, many years later, it pleased me to think that the young lovers shed a few tears. As we all know, memories are our finest creations. I did remember the church of Santa Croce, though, where I had admired Giotto's fresco of the death of St Francis of Assisi, surrounded by his disciples.

We were convinced that the soul didn't exist. It was an invention of primitive peoples. Nevertheless, the figure of the saint was continually in my thoughts.

Every night, I found myself kneeling before the recumbent figure. I was one of the monks around his catafalque. And I was praying. I was dreaming, needless to say, but the dream was very real. I stretched my hand out towards the smooth, lifeless face of the saint. I wept, and then woke up.

Vitalia.

I learnt that the night had claimed its share of victims. Thousands of dead taken in huge trains to be cremated. Vast pillars of smoke stained the sky. We were now living under permanent greyness. Our golden age had come to an end. Carthago was burning. We were the legions, we were Rome, and Scipio's dream went up in flames.

At night, I fell asleep, exhausted, and dreamt.

I'm lying against the cold wall of the chapel. Laid on a narrow catafalque. Monks are fingering my robe. Some are weeping. Others run their fingers lightly over my face. One of them has taken my hand in his. It is heavy, so heavy. Every surface of the world around me has entered an icy darkness.

VI

O N MY RETURN TO ROME, I read Sciascia in the dim light of my large room; it brought me some consolation for my fellow residents' stupidity and the terrible boredom that had come over me.

"Whose dream am I?" I wondered when reading the lines of the great Sicilian prose writer. "Am I the dream of this villa perched on the Pincio? Or of all the travellers who have come before me in the world order?"

But Sciascia was dreaming of me, the Arab from the tale:

"In his dream, he is surrounded by sand, a Sahara of black sand. There is no water, there is no sea. He is in the middle of a desert—in the desert you are always in the middle—and he is obsessed with trying to find a way out, when he sees someone next to him. Oddly enough, it is an Arab of the Bedouin tribes, mounted on a camel and holding a lance in his right hand. Under his left arm he has a stone; in that hand he holds a shell.

"The Arab tells him that his mission is to save the arts and sciences, and then brings the shell to his ear; the shell is extraordinarily beautiful. Wordsworth tells us he listened to the prophecy ('in an unknown tongue, which yet I understood'): a sort of impassioned ode prophesying that the earth was on the verge of being destroyed by a flood sent by the wrath of God. The Arab tells him that it is true, the flood is coming, but he has a mission:

to save the arts and sciences. He shows him the stone and, oddly, it is Euclid's *Elements*, while remaining a stone. Then he brings the shell closer and the shell too is a book; it is what has spoken those terrible things. The shell is, moreover, all the poetry of the world, including—why not?—the poem by Wordsworth. The Bedouin tells him: 'I must save these two things, the stone and the shell, both of them books.' He looks behind him, and there is a moment in which Wordsworth sees that the face of the Bedouin has changed, that it is full of horror. He too turns round and he sees a great light, which has flooded half the desert. This light is the light from the waters of the flood, which is about to submerge the earth. The Bedouin goes off and Wordsworth sees that he is also Don Quixote and that the camel is also Rosinante, and that in the same way as the stone was a book and the shell was a book, so the Bedouin is Don Quixote and is neither of the two and is both at once.

"Another thing to note in Wordsworth's nightmare is the terror inspired by the great light flooding the desert, which is said to be the light of the water. We know now that it might be something else because, for us, the image of atomic destruction has become indistinguishable from the image of a universal flood. We should also note that the image of Don Quixote resolutely riding away recalls that particular painting by Daumier, perhaps of the exact same moment."

Don Quixote leant over to tell me the adventures of my double, the other Sinbad, who lived more than a thousand years ago and whose journey continued in the memory of women storytellers; and I listened, just as fascinated as Sinbad the Landsman, the Porter who long ago entered the home of my double by chance.

It was a strange encounter in Baghdad, an ironic twist of fate; two men of the same age, speaking the same language and bearing the same name, twins separated by their stations in life: one made wealthy by a life of adventure, the other poor as Job.

And I pictured myself too in Sinbad the Sailor's luxurious house, surrounded by women slender as ephebes, free and sweet as flowers, wild as fawns. Exhausted by a day of hard labour carrying my load through the famous markets of Baghdad, which were the envy of the world, I finally rested in the dim light so conducive to storytelling, that dream liberated by words. As I was being presented with dishes of fine food—which I enjoyed greatly—my host told me of his strange life.

Baghdad was a mirage that had materialized in the desert, like those oases which split in two in the heat of the sands and encourage twice as many daydreams in the shade of palm trees by murmuring streams. It was a town impossible to loot, and yet it was looted, and so badly that virtually no trace of it remained except in the memory of its descendants who, to ensure they would never forget, spread wondrous stories which, unlike the town, would live on for ever. And so Sinbad would travel the seas for eternity, tethered to a painter's canvas like Odysseus to his mast, his arms bound but his mind full of harmonies, depicted against a background blue as the sea at night, a captive on a crescent-shaped boat.

And Harun-al-Rashid, Commander of the Faithful, disguised himself as a beggar to spy on his subjects and learn of their hopes and disappointments. At night, he would slip like an alley cat into sleazy taverns where men drank wine with an unknown quantity of thieves, even though it was often said that there were in fact forty of them, and that they had fabulous riches hidden in a cave; this would open when they uttered *simsim*, a mysterious word like a cascade of silver coins that was to fire the imaginations of generations of children, captains of the night standing at the prow of a dream. The real caliph, dressed as a poor wretch, watched a huge illuminated boat floating past on the Tigris. They were honouring Caliph Harun-al-Rashid, a man who was passing himself off as him, the Commander of the Faithful. His double was living a life of gaudy splendour and luxury in Baghdad, as one might imagine, and, as might be expected of a great prince, was decked out in great finery like a woman, a forerunner of the usurpers who were to corrupt and ruin the beautiful city before it was laid waste to by the Mongolian armies.

And the beggar prince watched the bogus caliph pass by like an idol that had to be burnt, shivering in horror at the thought of what would eventually become of all this power, which was nothing but a magical yet destructive masquerade, a grotesque farce that would destroy both story and storyteller.

And Sinbad listened to him, hungry for adventures and desperate for rest, dozing in the subdued light of a palace where—in a courtyard bathed with light—a fountain sobbed.

Amid tears, songs and laughter, a man like any other crossed seas and battled with fabulous animals; he encountered biblical fish that fed flocks, and continents on which the distant descendants of caravaneers had been shipwrecked. The caravaneers ruled the seas and dropped anchor beside the islands of Java or Sumatra, or the Islands of the Moon, which were governed by playing-card kings, interchangeable figures who rode horses from the sea, strange creatures born of sea spray and wave.

And Sinbad the Porter clung tight to the talons of the giant bird, the Rukh, during a dream brought on by the opium he'd eaten in the sweetmeats served up by the real Sinbad, who was master of this strange ceremony. He flew over mountains and oceans, overcame his fear, and came back to Baghdad even richer, where

74

he surrounded himself with his kin, a brotherhood of hashish-smokers whose gossip inspired the hordes of storytellers appearing in all the souks of the round city which, in the year 1000, boasted a million inhabitants. It was the biggest city in the world.

VII

INFLUENCED by what I was reading, I dreamt comically that I was the destroyer of the Eternal City. It was as if I wanted to punish the poor inhabitants of this sleepy little town in modern Italy for my dismal isolation in the company of a madwoman who designed stage sets and was desperate for me to take Italian lessons; a painter cursed with the improbable name of Michelangelo—poor sod—who fervently messed about with colours in his studio; an art historian, Jean Dubois, who indulged in vices worthy of a Borgia; and a dissonant musician, Diego the Portuguese. Not forgetting Jeanne and Pauline, two writers captivated by ugliness and triviality whose work, which bored me to tears, was destined for a bright literary future, despite the fact that they'd only just begun it, and Federico Di Lano, an occasional poet, a born artist and the only Italian out of that group who knew a little French.

Federico was always hanging around Michelangelo and he used to sit in on the dauber's lengthy work sessions. The latter was trying to reproduce the exact shade of Rome, his holy grail, the slightly dirty ochre of the city's façades. He'd bought metres and metres of canvas for his black work, then had hung them in his studio and had covered them in a rusty colour. He lived in the hope of one day exhibiting the fruit of his alchemical quest in a New York gallery.

I really don't want to provide a longer list of the men and women who made my life a living hell. It's enough to give you an overview and, anyway, I only remember the most famous ones. The people whom the world will still be talking about in centuries to come. For that matter, who knows what has become of them? I sit here in this gloomy room in Carthago talking to you, and I have no idea where they are today. You make up all kinds of stories, you delude yourself about people, you imagine that you think and feel the same as them, that you share their hopes and dreams in some way. Wrong: you're way off base: former acquaintances fade away in the golden twilight of our lives. All those weirdos are nothing but shadows now. They could be at the height of their fame, but I, the man from Carthago, wouldn't even sense their presence—it would be even less real than yours, my lord, or that of your dog with its putrid breath.

It would have been a great help to have had Robinson there! With his feet firmly on the ground and his head in the stars, he would have been able to sort out this world of smoke and mirrors. Naturally, I did go back to the Corso, but there wasn't any trace of that purveyor of fascist posters. I asked other Africans doing the same job where he was, but all I got were shrugs, vague directions and far-fetched stories about the tall Senegalese being picked up by a rich Roman woman and given board and lodging, with silk bed sheets, in exchange for his manly attentions: "After all, my brother, everyone knows that we Africans are more energetic in the sack than you Arabs; it's true, brother, obviously you've got a little African in you, but you aren't black and you've spent too much time mixing with those Toubabs, who've got no balls, my friend, and that's a fact"—and they all shouted with laughter on the Corso, annoying the good people of Rome with their loud, joyful guffaws.

But there was Vitalia, or, rather, the memory of Vitalia to cheer me up or drive me to despair when I felt lonely. Vitalia, whose breath swept me along on the crest of dreams, at the vanguard of my youthful socialism, at the time when the mad leaders of my country had decided to mongrelize the revolution by adding a dash of Islam to strengthen the two ideologies. This had resulted in the death of the first and such a rebirth of the second that it had become the ultimate taboo to talk about love in Carthago. I countered the traumatic effects this had on me by falling madly in love with the first woman to appear on the scene. Vitalia was the victim of all my frustrations.

In the meantime, Jeanne and Pauline showed me a good time, since the two authoresses were not averse to the games of love. Those Amazons came onto me at night, when Giovanna was on duty with that old fool of a director. I tiptoed to their room, tapped on their door, pulled out the peg and the latch fell. One of the noble maidens, Pauline—the taller, thinner and blonder—pulled me onto the bed where they both slept, naked as children, though their hips and breasts were broad as splayed fans, and, sandwiching me between their hot bodies, they examined me thoroughly. This intricate threesome was a strange kind of loving; I investigated one, while the other set about me. I was a plaything of flesh and nerves, a harp, a zither, a woman, in their expert hands, under their aggressive lips and insinuating tongues. I surrendered my manhood and let Jeanne and Pauline invade me. I had never before experienced such indecency from fingers and eyes as they played with me, forcing me to adopt strange positions. This may seem odd to mere mortals who have never come across the kind of love in which the person who thinks he's calling all the shots isn't. At times they seized my cock and sucked me off, then made me enter the opening of the woman who was the more attractive of the two, but not the more submissive. Then they'd neglect me, abandoning me on the side of the bed while they had fun on

79

their own, a sight which could have brought a dead man back to life and which more than made up for being left to my own devices. I played with myself while they brazenly went down on each other, laughing and moaning quietly, and this was how it went on for most of the night, before they again ganged up on me, pouncing like lionesses on their poor prey who was bristling with a monumental erection—I'm generous towards my own anatomy, God helps those who help themselves—anyway, the amorous hussies impaled themselves by turns on my mast, moving faster and faster, one on my lower abdomen, the other on my face or bruised mouth; they had barely broken into a sweat, while I was almost dead, but happy, and then they came over my cock, my balls, my stomach, as I shot my load in turn like a hanged man. It's hardly surprising, really, that I went over every other evening to help Jeanne and Pauline write another page of their intimate novel. They were loving and indispensable company for me, as was Giovanna who also possessed hidden treasures which, unfortunately, she had no wish to share with the twins, out of fear or distrust of Sapphic love.

———

O NE EVENING, I attend the wedding of one of the Golem's members of staff. The family has hired the Villa Medici for the wedding party.

Women in evening dresses, men wearing tails, all of them from Naples, Federico tells me.

Big band, forties jazz music: Glenn Miller. Boring.

I slip on a jacket and dark trousers and gatecrash the wedding. At the end of the evening, a man dressed in white with enormous, blue-tinted glasses, comes up on stage in front of the band and begins singing. He must be in his sixties or seventies at least.

According to Federico, he's an Italian singer who hasn't appeared on stage for twenty-five years.

"He's famous," explains Federico, "for his connections with the Italian and American mafia."

The old man sings two or three songs, applauded by the guests who are singing along to the choruses. He even dances a couple of waltz steps with a buxom woman in a red dress. He leaves the stage just as quickly and disappears. I feel like I'm watching the beginning of *The Godfather*.

The band goes back to playing old American standards. No one is dancing. Except the lady in red, who has nothing to lose. The Italians don't spend a lot of time on dance floors. They don't like making an exhibition of themselves. Just like they don't swim when they're on the beach. They sunbathe. In Rome, you have to keep yourself to yourself if you want to make a good impression.

It's two o'clock in the morning. The party is over. Jean Dubois, Michelangelo and I head into Rome. Dubois has an old car that his parents gave him.

Jean Dubois is your stereotypical Villa resident: Catholic, from a good family, and married, he spends happy days at the Villa where he can pretend to be an artist. Anyway, on Sundays, he immerses himself in his painting, with a straw hat perched on his head. He and his friend Diego, the Portuguese musician, bring girls up to his room where they and Diego display their prowess while Dubois sketches them. Sometimes Jeanne and Pauline join in, but they often forgo the pleasure when they see the surprise guests. Diego and Dubois, who aren't very choosy, tend to pick up pretty much anyone hanging around the Villa.

"Life is beautiful!" yells Jean Dubois, driving his sports car at speed through the night.

The Colosseum, the Arch of Septimius Severus, the Palatine Hill, the Pyramid of Cestius, the Via Appia and the Baths of Caracalla flash by.

I remember a day spent inside the high walls of the baths built by Caracalla, an absolute monarch who was as formidable as you'd expect from a "barely integrated barbarian", words you might hear these days from French nationalists. People also had concerns in ancient times and, although Arabs who have since become Muslims are now feared in France, at that time people were suspicious of Orientals and Africans. It didn't matter whether the finest achievements of the Roman Empire dated from the reign of Caracalla or not; people preferred the refined barbarism of Hadrian, who ordered the execution of the architect of the Pantheon. Septimius Severus—Caracalla's father, who was born in Libya, at Leptis Magna, and whose majestic arch leads into the Forum, where you can still enjoy wandering aimlessly among the ancient stones—came under fire for the same thing. Another uncultured African on the Roman throne, what a scandal for historians of the century of colonialism!

So I strolled inside the walls of the baths where every Roman had come to bathe, irrespective of social class, and I wondered whether the slaves came here together with their masters. I walked beside the stone cliffs, through the rooms beneath a pure, empty sky, and over the ancient mosaics. Then I sat down to fantasize about the glory which was sure to welcome me with open arms on my return to Carthago. A futile daydream, as I later discovered.

Another magical place in Rome, where I could forget the din of the town, was the Palatine Hill. This hanging garden, this vast mirror to time, is such a pleasant place to walk that I imagined myself a poet of the same stature as Goethe, depicted in some amateurish painting with a hat on his head, a blade of grass in his mouth, sitting languidly in the shade of a cypress tree, here on the Palatine Hill, meditating on the end of civilization. It was really the only spot in Rome where you could relax, and it was always a place of refuge for me when my love for Vitalia was tearing me apart.

So you can imagine my surprise when I saw Robinson there, selling postcards, dressed as a gladiator.

"What are you doing here? The sailor has come ashore! What a laugh!"

"I've been looking for you everywhere. I asked after you on the Corso. No one knew where you were hiding."

"My dear Sinbad, I met a woman… and what a woman! A Roman from the Piazza di Spagna, Via Marghutta. The love of my life…"

"How old?"

"Love doesn't care how old a woman is, if she's from a good family. Anyway, how old is your Vitalia?"

"Er…"

"See, you scoundrel… I, on the other hand, pick a mature woman who is comfortable in her Prada shoes and who has a downcast arse but a cheerful purse. And I enjoy sweet fragrances, like our Prophet, Mohammed; as well as women."

Robinson was Senegalese and, what's more, a Tijani, from the Sufi brotherhood that had produced many wise men. Robinson must have been its final representative. He'd inherited the calm, slow religiosity of a shepherd from his ancestors.

"What has happened to your Roman lady?" I asked.

"She hung herself."

"Oh, I'm very sorry to hear that, very… sorry…"

Robinson threw back his head and laughed dementedly, which was shocking in the circumstances. He was crazy.

"She hung herself around another black man's neck! What did you think I meant? That she committed suicide? That'll be the day. Women never give themselves a hard time! All we are to them is doormats to be beaten this way and that. Look at you, poor sod, you're pining for a little slut who doesn't give a damn about you. Or you're being used as a vibrator by your Giovanna and God knows who else in that villa."

"What about you, Robinson, aren't you sick of making an exhibition of yourself dressed up as a gladiator? That is, when you're not selling pictures of Il Duce's ugly mug."

"I'm being pushed to these terrible extremes by African poverty. Look where rampant national stupidity in Algeria has got you."

"We can't blame our motherlands for everything!"

"What else can we do, colonialism no longer sells. You can't blame the Whites, the Pieds-Noirs, the French army or the paratroopers any more. They decamped fifty years ago."

"Without those criminals, things might have been a little more peaceful back in the old country. Two centuries of colonization is the kiss of death for a continent, Robinson! You can't deny that. Not to mention slavery."

"I'm not a slave, Sinbad. No more hassle, no more cotton fields, cudgels and whips. It's the same for you Algerians: your *Frenchies* have gone. What exactly are you waiting for before waking up and sounding the clarion call for development? You have the oil, the women activists and the men to start the turbines! All you do is kill each other instead of avenging the honour of Africa, avenging the insult."

Good old Robinson was right. We were living in the hell created by our unsuccessful attempts at independence. We got bogged down, so we fled to the other side of the world to live off the scraps thrown by our former masters. Why? No reason, just to have a bit more fun before the big sleep. But, more than anything, I wanted to preserve that unique, affectionate, loving faith inside me that embraced all that life possessed of beauty: women and their unassailable youth, reflected in a mirror held up to combat nothingness. I sought consolation in Giovanna's arms the way I had sought consolation in Vitalia's arms, well aware that this would also come to an end one day, and that I would have to put out to sea again and drift; a life without destiny, a bundle cast onto the waves and carried away by wind and tide, and icy currents, and weary death.

Often, at night, alone again in my bed after love's embraces, I conjured up Vitalia's face and the old sorrow surged through me. Why did that girl haunt me so? We'd barely spoken to each other: the only language we'd known was making the beast with two backs. Of course, the little flirt had taught me a few words of Italian. I knew how to fuck in the language of Dante but I still didn't know Vitalia's hopes and dreams, I didn't know how old she was, even though I had a feeling that she was no older than Proust's young girls in flower. She came back every evening and stood at the foot of my bed like an ancient heroine giving herself to her lover, weary of a long courtship, burning like a flame, but just as fitful, so I had to take her in the space of a breath, in case she was blown out.

VIII

O NE NIGHT, I heard someone knocking at the door of my room. I opened it to find a tall man dressed in black standing there, silent as an apparition. He was wearing a stained, wide-brimmed felt hat that had seen better days.

"I'm a painter."

"You can call me Sinbad."

"The real Sinbad? The Sailor? It's an honour."

He took my hand and shook it as if he were trying to work it loose.

"My name's Ingres. I've been thinking about you for years while I was painting. I was brought up on your adventures."

No one ever knows the effect they have on other people, and even though I didn't really understand, I still felt flattered.

"My adventures?"

"Sinbad, your voyages are famous. The adventures of Sinbad the Seaman. All the children in the world know who you are."

"I don't understand."

"The moving island? The Rukh bird? The monkey-men and the giant who roasted men? The pit of the dead? The old man of the sea? The valley of diamonds? The golden voyage? Your last. Don't tell me you don't remember!"

"Well... no, I don't."

"I thought as much! This shabby residence! This accursed villa! It's hell. People disappear into here and forget who they are."

Although the fuss he was making and his exclamations sounded put on or overdone, my evening visitor seemed in earnest. He was gazing at me as if I were the embodiment of an old dream. He took my hand as if holding a child's hand and talked about Sinbad's adventures—my adventures.

He told me the story of Sinbad the Sailor who invited Sinbad the Porter to dine in his huge house, pretty much the same way I've brought you here to the house of my grandmother, Lalla Fatima, to tell you the story of my life.

To my amazement, Sinbad the Sailor, my oriental double, embarked on the tale of his voyages, his shipwrecks, his dramatic downfalls and his spectacular fortunes. And I, Sinbad the Porter, listened as if trying to fathom my double's soul and gaze at my reflection in a shifting mirror of words.

"I inherited considerable property from my father, the greater part of which I squandered in my youth on a life of dissipation, but I soon realized the error of my ways and reflected that riches did not last long when mismanaged in such a way. I also reflected that my irregular lifestyle had led me to fritter away my time, which is the most precious thing of all.

"And I thought that being poor in old age was the worst and most regrettable of all misfortunes. I remembered noble Solomon's saying: 'The grave is better than want.'

"So I gathered together what remained of my fortune and sold all my goods and chattels by public auction in Baghdad's market. This was easy to do since the town of Caliph Harun-al-Rashid was also the home of the merchants whose stalls surrounded the palace of the Commander of the Faithful. Baghdad was laid out in concentric circles like an astrolabe. It was as round as the moon. In this town, I met some merchants who travelled the seas and who were excellent men. They had a haughty demeanour, wore moustaches and shaved their beards, which wasn't the custom in our country; they flouted the laws of hospitality, too, because they never lodged with their fellow merchants in Baghdad, preferring to stay in *fonduks*, those strange inns where you might meet every kind of creature on the good Lord's earth. Having struck up a friendship with several of these rogues, I left for Basra where I boarded one of their vessels.

"We set sail, steering our course towards the country of Hind.

"During our voyage, we landed at several islands, where we sold or exchanged our goods. One day, while under sail, we were becalmed near a small island, which was not much higher than the level of the water and looked like a meadow. The captain ordered his sails to be furled and allowed anyone to go on shore who wished to do so; I was one of those who disembarked. But while we were enjoying drinking copious amounts of wine, eating abundant dried meats and salted fruits, and swimming through azure waters to the distant horizon and then back to rest on this welcoming shore, the island suddenly shook with a terrible tremor. What we had thought was an island was the back of a whale. The quickest and most agile of us escaped in the rowboat or threw themselves into the sea and swam back to the ship; I was held back by the waves, and so saw the captain hoist his sails and continue his voyage, leaving me to my fate.

"I struggled against the elements for two days and two nights. On the morning of the third day, exhausted and in danger of being claimed by the wine-dark sea, I was lifted by a huge wave and tossed onto the shore, like Odysseus on the island of the Phaeacians. But I was even more alone than industrious Odysseus, the man of a thousand turns, since there was no Nausicaa waiting to lead me to her people.

"I fell asleep, my strength gone, for a very long time.

"I was ravenously hungry when I woke up, so I went in search of food. But all I found were pasturelands grazed by huge horses;

I was already picturing myself capturing and eating them when a man suddenly appeared from under the earth, as in those ludicrous old stories.

"The man asked me who I was and I told him all about my misfortunes. I think he took pity on me because he led me into a cave, where several other people were waiting. He introduced me to them and they prepared a meal for me, which revived me. These men were the grooms of a certain Mirage, whom they said was their king. They had come to this island with the king's mares, which they tied to pickets on the shore to wait for stallions from the sea to cover them and impregnate them. Then, before these sea stallions could devour the mares, the men would come out of their hiding places, shouting to frighten away the terrible sea creatures, which would return to Poseidon. The mares impregnated in this fashion were taken back to the king. There they gave birth to sea horses that were azure and silver like the waves, fearsome in war and faster at the gallop than the best horses on earth.

"Once their work was finished, the grooms took me to their island and presented me to King Mirage, whose kingdom, despite being illusory, numbered thousands of islands scattered over a vast sea. While I was waiting for people from my own land to arrive, the king showered me with costly gifts and, in return, I told him the story of my life and described the disaster that had almost cost my life and had resulted in my exile. I had been lucky in my misfortune; unlike illustrious Odysseus, I had no wife or son. Penelope wasn't waiting for me beside her loom, and Telemachus wasn't attacking youths of his own age at the risk of losing his life or, worse, his reason.

"Then, one day, the ship that had abandoned me to the waves dropped anchor by King Mirage's island. When I managed to convince them that I was the one and only Sinbad, not a ghost or, worse, an imposter—of whom there will be many more, I fear,

as my life and novel travel through the centuries—the captain
gave me back my goods and agreed to take me on board. Before
I left, King Mirage showered me with many gifts and I returned
to Baghdad even richer than before."

IX

B UT SINBAD was getting away from the storyteller, the man in the big hat who claimed to be a painter of odalisques, just as he'd once got away from the monkey-man who was going to roast him on a spit and eat him: he'd gouged out that monster's eyes just as Odysseus had done to his Cyclops, and had escaped with his companions by hanging from the fleece of a sheep. And the painter of idols watched him disappear into the distance towards Basra, returning at last, experienced and knowledgeable, to die among his own people, a figure larger than the story trying to imprison him.

Sinbad was immortal: he was reborn with every new generation and reincarnated as a young man with a wayfaring soul, his bag empty and his eyes filled with wonders, who always washed up in a foreign town with incomprehensible customs, just as he himself had washed up on a beach and had been picked up by a young woman with burning, salty skin. But the picture that the great Ingres intended to paint frightened me to death. I was terrified of ending up imprisoned by the canvas the way Giovanna had been by the Academy's elderly director, Paduzzi di Balto.

So, with an entirely oriental gentleness, I sent the spectre in the floppy hat packing and closed the door behind him. I could breathe freely again at last; my heartbeat could return to normal and my mind could rest easy after all that excitement. I'd had more than enough of the Villa, its residents and its illustrious dead; even Giovanna was exhausting me with her obsessive sexual demands. I sorted out my things. I didn't have much, just a few shirts, a couple of pairs of trousers, and some socks and boxer shorts. I opened a suitcase and threw the lot inside.

Like my illustrious ancestor, the Sinbad of legend, I boarded a ship at Genoa, not Basra, and sailed along the coast to Messina in Sicily. The crossing was short and the voyage comfortable, compared to my earlier one. This was a ferry, not a fishing boat, and no one was in danger of dying of thirst or ending up at the bottom of the sea or, worse, locked up in a humanitarian-aid camp. So I allowed myself to drift for a night, sitting in an armchair, surrounded by the snoring of other passengers and the soft lapping of the sea.

Messina was a strange, ugly town, built beside the straits.

A stroll by the sea yielded a certain transient charm, particularly when thinking about Odysseus trying to avoid being caught between Scylla and Charybdis. Sinbad the sailor was trying to find the channel which would let him continue his voyage to Ithaca. This was yet another of his old stories which was of interest to no one except a few elderly scholars locked in a library's forbidden-book section. The youth of today preferred new technology to ancient knowledge. Who could blame them? Wasn't it better to download mindless music than read the *Odyssey*? Or chat to people all over the world without ever getting to know them properly—which was preferable really—instead of getting lost in the pages of a book with fanatical egocentricity.

People wanted to be connected with everyone at all costs. The only thing limiting the virtual universe was its own virtuality. The most effective, most lethal prisons were those we created for ourselves with a computer, an Internet connection and a total indifference to reality. An ignorant disregard for the rest of the planet. People had friends all over the world but had never met any of them. People carried on passionate relationships with strangers who could alter their sex and identity at will. You could take part in a protest for Tibet or Afghanistan just by clicking on a link, forgetting that the torturers were employing a harder kind of technology that bore little relation to software.

Anyone could influence a foreign government that didn't allow its subjects to access this marvel of technology and instantaneous information, just by adding their names to an online petition.

Proteus, the shape-changing God, was master of this global sham.

Contemporary tastes therefore required a permanent presence, a perpetual state of wakefulness, but one without quality or flavour. Modern man simply had to be able to absorb all this pointless knowledge and be in possession of an elephantine memory to do so. Even a 100MB hard disk was more valuable than an active brain. Odysseus was now reduced to a computer virus, a Trojan Horse, a vicious line of code that had to be deleted as fast as possible. The man of a thousand turns was consigned to the past because there was no processor fast enough to cope with him.

The god known as Norton naturally watched over the unassailable Troy of our futile capacities, the thousands of hours vaporized by watching amorphous images, reading aimless lines and, just like geese, gobbling up scraps of information provided by our Aeolus. Online newspapers were a lot of hot air; no one read them any more anyway, and the serious press was dying, unable to compete with games, music for free—the magic word of the century—and video on demand. Keeping informed was easy with all those blogs that allowed everyone to air their views about nothing. This e-commerce café was a serious danger to the planet's mental health. The future of democracy was a never-ending debate somewhere on the Net.

This huge knowledge base was no use to anyone and, what was worse, it made people powerless; they stored the data so that it was even easier for them to ignore it. In this way, the human race was merrily preparing to take a giant leap into oblivion.

Messina was very similar to this new world. The city had been struck by a great tidal wave early in the last century and had been rebuilt on top of the ruins of the baroque town. Baroque had been abandoned in favour of the 1900s style—everything that was attractive and new in the early twentieth century. But, after Poseidon, Mars came along and devastated the terrible city. American bombers reduced it to ashes in the Second World War.

It was rebuilt again. Hastily.

Now it looked faded, dreary and tacky, like the last in a long line of reproductions. Its soul was dead. No doubt its inhabitants, tired of so many disasters, weren't about to build anything to last. They had to be able to take it down before the next performance; to change the scenery before the tragedy.

I'd lived in Carthago for many years, another disaster-ridden town, so Messina was a city after my own heart. It touched anyone who was disenchanted or nostalgic for gory comedies. I was continually reliving a wretched past as I walked its streets. I was strolling through the kingdom of the dead. Anyway, the inhabitants of Messina were the saddest people in Sicily. They were waiting, with a certain amount of trepidation, for the bridge promised by the Golem that would link the tip of Calabria to their sunken city.

I might well have tired of so much misery if I hadn't met Liza.

She was a receptionist at the hotel where I was staying. She was wearing a wedding ring, which was the first thing I noticed, since I hadn't yet experienced adultery. I soon remedied this oversight, since we found ourselves together in the same room one evening when it was raining, the hotel was deserted and its guests seemed to have disappeared into the city's limbo.

Liza was slender as a reed, a pale yellow reed like the ones my father and I used for making fishing rods. Back then, we had to suspend the long pole over the fire and heat it so that it acquired the flexibility and strength needed for the hazardous activity of fishing on the shores of Carthago at night, or at daybreak when the sun, still below the horizon, illuminates the water which turns emerald, then clear. At that precise moment, the sea would fill with fish and the rods, embedded in the sand and topped by a little bell, would snap in half with a tinkling of bells to signal a bite. We would then frantically race over to seize the long rod and land the fish.

I would remember those mornings by the sea as I held Liza in my arms. The young woman trembled like the taut line linking the catch to the fisherman. Highly charged, she was shaking like a leaf, so badly that, to calm her, I told her about those nights with my father on the long beaches of Carthago, where the Romans once landed before torching the city. But Liza burned even hotter than the ramparts of that trading city, she was set on fire by my caresses, while I went under like a siren embraced by an Odysseus who wasn't so tightly bound to his ship. What kind of adventure would the famous sailor have had if he'd been prepared to join the sirens singing for him? Man will never know and will always daydream about this missed encounter.

The child I once was would have let himself be carried off in the arms of the women who sang so well, just as in Messina, trapped between Liza's thighs, netted by her breathing and her song, quivering like a sea bream or leer fish hooked on a line, I was held captive by the will of a woman tense as the breaking day and relentless as a kiss. Adultery is the song of the sirens, drifting slowly with endless patience, knowing that you will eventually lose your life or your soul. No one gave Liza any love now in Messina—a cold, dead town stuck in a past filled with bombing raids and earthquakes—so she preferred to lose her soul there: it was one way of proving she still had one.

I explored her stomach like a new shore and kissed her small breasts that flushed red under my tongue. Then she reared, like a caught fish which refuses to surrender and thrashes about, then escapes, fluid and silvery. Between Liza's damp thighs, on top of her stomach, flat as the shores of Sirte, I wondered how to escape the catastrophe brewing beneath the caresses and murmurs. My warped sailor's mind continued to hold onto the pure, intact image of Vitalia who, like a Penelope, was my one true love, my talisman against the sweetest of evil charms, like a fiery wife whose singing is both sheer delight and sheer torture.

Liza, like Beatrice, didn't try to stop me leaving when, one morning, I picked up my suitcase and left the hotel, kissing her slender hand one last time. My memories of that husbandless wife were tender yet bitter. She'd brought back my childhood and the image of a father who'd disappeared among the sirens, blinded by the cold, metallic brilliance of the sea, a shattered mirror that would last till the end of time. Perhaps my ongoing desire for travel and for women should be regarded as a discreet homage to the father who'd strayed after mistaking false love for the one true love? If only my mother hadn't died, abandoning her Odysseus to all kinds of pretenders, vandals and murderers, to the Calypsos and Circes who inhabited the infernal regions of this world and who brandished unrealistic promises and sang glorious songs, cold as the seabed. I was soon left an orphan, raised by my grandmother among mirages and cock-and-bull stories, soothed often by foolish dreams while Carthago foundered, sinking into barbarism.

———

I TRAVELLED TO SYRACUSE. I liked the town, which made me feel strangely lethargic. I felt that I could breathe more freely walking through the narrow lanes, over the Piazza del Duomo, strolling along the boardwalk, a balcony suspended over the ocean, the dream of sailors or merchants setting out on expeditions for a thousand years. But, like a wife or an abandoned whore, I stayed on the quay, gazing into the dream-filled depths. I imagined Archimedes erecting his mirrors to burn the Roman ships, a popular legend that had been masquerading as truth since time immemorial. It was a wonder that men seemed to prefer tall stories to tangible proof, even if it was dry as straw. They preferred the mystery of the heavens to the mathematical order of the world.

I also remembered the Arabs who invited themselves to Syracuse in the ninth century, when they were still sailing on strange, fragile crafts that could cross oceans, as Sinbad, the one from the legend, liked to relate.

I tried to forget my loneliness, the strange, nagging impression that I was continually reliving the same things, as if my story belonged to everyone. I travelled, but everyone travelled. I went from one woman to the next in search of Vitalia, but everyone spent their life like this, moving from one embrace to another, from one face to another, mistaking the image of love for true love and ending up with nothing. People grew old, their memories faded, they finished their lives alone and went to the grave and eternal oblivion. Life is nothing. An illusion. Like the ever-moving waves pulsing in the light.

I would have liked to be wrong, to believe in an afterlife, something to make up for all the sorrow we experience in life. The worst part was thinking that everything we'd lived through had been in vain and would disappear with the death of that vessel of marvels or sorrows, the demise of the person of flesh and feathers: body, dreams, mind and desires which had once been in the light and were now conspicuous by their absence. The Sailor's true wealth resided in his good fortune in being able to reinvent himself through his women and his voyages; and if there was no rhyme or reason to that, if it were just free verse, just poetry doomed to be scattered to the wind like an ephemeral word, then who cared? The important thing was not to be weighed down by baggage—you had to travel light, taking only the bare minimum for moral comfort.

I walked to the Piazza del Duomo and sat down at a table in a café facing the cathedral, which had been built around a Greek temple. I was ordering a lemonade, when suddenly a tall, very dark man appeared: Robinson hadn't changed, he might have put on a little weight, but I wasn't sure. He almost looked taller than usual. He was dressed in the latest fashion.

"My dear Robinson, you look so affluent… a three-piece suit, in this frightful heat?"

"Elegance makes no allowances for the weather, Sinbad! Clothes maketh a man, particularly a black man."

"Fine clothes do not make a gentleman."

"We'd be hung if we dressed as we used to do in the village, me wearing a *bubu* and you a *gandura*. You and your lousy proverbs, only savages like you attach credence to…"

"Still on form, I see. So you left your patch of pavement in Rome?"

"Those Lazio bastards were driving me crazy. I was always having to run away from them. And when I'd outdistanced them, the *carabinieri* took over. You know, those clowns in fancy dress who think they're policemen and pick up tourists."

"And what are you up to now, Robinson?"

"I'm working for the honourable Carlo Moro."

I almost jumped out of my skin. I didn't expect to come across Vitalia's father again.

"He's a good man," added the Negro.

"He almost killed me."

"You assaulted the virgin he'd raised as his daughter."

"As his daughter?"

"She isn't his daughter."

"His niece, then?"

"His wife!"

I fell to the ground like a stone dropped from a great height by those wretched birds who flew to Mecca's aid in the Qur'an.

"The free spirit is lost for words! I've silenced the joker, the gossip, the man of legend! That makes me very happy. I'm working for the husband who is a pillar of respectable society."

"So they employ…"

"*Naturellement.* These descendants of slave-traders aren't racists, you know. I say 'descendants' because you know a thing or two about that, don't you, Sinbad."

"I'm not going to feel guilty for the crimes of my ancestors, Robinson. The Arabs already have quite enough on their plate with their disastrous present without wasting time worrying about their ancestors' slave-trading past."

"But if you look at your cousins in Saudi…"

"What fool would go back to Mecca and stick their hand in the royal wasps' nest? You'd have to be as poor as a Pakistani to do that!"

"You'd have to be really naive to take a cargo of that kind of coal to the home of Abdullah!"

"But what can you tell me about Vitalia?"

"You good-for-nothing sailor!"

"I…"

"Wooooooooh, he's in love!" exclaimed Robinson. "Carlo's flighty wife is running around in search of a sailor."

"Is that true?"

"Cut off my hand in Arabia if it's not. She's been confiding in me since she found out that we're friends before God. She's told me over and over how much she misses you."

At those words, I jumped up and hugged Robinson with tears in my eyes.

"She's waiting for you in Palermo. She asked me to take you to her. I'm risking my Negro neck for your sex life, Sinbad. If that's not friendship, I don't know what is!"

"Shall we go?"

"Come on, then!"

X

I WAS REUNITED with Vitalia in Palermo. Robinson came up with a clever scheme to tell her I was there and she agreed to see me again. I was to wait for her in the church of the Martorana. I waited, my heart aflame, my soul liquefied, and she came. She'd changed, her face had lost the radiance and roundness of the first flush of youth, but I thought she was even more attractive. Beneath the Byzantine mosaics, beneath the fire and the gold, her dark hair acquired Venetian-red highlights that filled me with wonder.

We went out into the Kalsa, the Arab quarter, where it was easy to hide from prying eyes. We thought we'd be shielded by the narrow lanes. She took me to a bombed-out chapel that hadn't been restored after the war. Much as it pains me, I can't now remember its name. It had a melancholy atmosphere. The high walls standing open to the sky, over the altar, were symbolic of our love. Boundless freedom and the vivacious brilliance of youth, which had begun on a beach and continued here, under the dazzling skies of Sicily, where I renewed my acquaintance with Sciascia and the enjoyment afforded by his books.

I took Vitalia in my arms and embraced her on the altar—a strange communion—and even though she was married, I felt as if I were marrying her. When I told her so, she reminded me that I was an Arab, and a Muslim to boot. She slipped her tongue in my mouth to mollify me, but the bite of her words hurt even more.

The glare of the sea, my memories of the beach, her sea-surf body, I remembered it all and it made me want to cry. Separated for decades, we were now old lovers trying to relive our lost youth. Which might have been true if her caresses hadn't become more insistent in the meantime and if her burning, trembling body weren't reminding me with every second that she was as alive as running water, and that we were young.

Then we entered the garden amidst the flames. I was becoming a mystic, with my thoughts of the bombs and fires that had set this Eden ablaze. In the scorching heat of the sun, I became capable of all forms, all images, as Ibn 'Arabi had. When I took her in my arms again, we were already dancing like stars under the canopy of heaven. Or perhaps it was the constantly spinning earth that was waltzing with us?

In the end, we decided to leave Palermo together and get as far away as possible from this town and Carlo Moro.

This time I had to wait for her in the Monreale cloister, just above Palermo. It was a safe place and the custodian would open the gates of the park for me. Vitalia had already paid him the *pizzo* through Robinson. The tall Senegalese knew all the Sicilian dodges. Anyway, the cloister, which was stunningly beautiful, had gardens overlooking the bay of Palermo and an Arab-Norman church, whose ceilings were covered with Byzantine mosaics.

The cloister was supported by pairs of columns, covered in gold inlay and arabesques. Walking beneath the spectacular vault of the Duomo di Monreale while waiting for Vitalia that day, I experienced the unique pleasure of listening to the acanthus leaves pressed against the flowering capitals, as the light danced like a spirit from that world.

She was late, she wasn't coming, I was going crazy. We'd decided to escape by sea. To take a boat. When I had worked myself into a state of complete despair, I saw Robinson rushing towards me, out of breath, his face drawn with tiredness.

"Sinbad, I've got some bad news."

He fell silent.

"Speak to me, Robinson, speak to me!"

"Vitalia…"

"Has something happened to her?"

Robinson looked at me as if I were the sorriest wretch in the whole world, as if I deserved his deepest pity.

"She's dead, Sinbad."

The world was thrown off its axis and the daylight vanished. Darkness descended on the cloister and the columns blurred.

"What! You're lying. You're mad!"

Robinson wasn't lying. The custodian had alerted Carlo Moro that his wife, Vitalia, had paid him to leave the cloister gates open. And he'd seen her with a tall black man. Carlo Moro then had Robinson followed and he found out Vitalia's little game, although he didn't understand the ins and outs of it. He saw her sorting her things, packing a suitcase and withdrawing money from the bank. He concluded that she was leaving with Robinson. Beside himself with jealousy, he'd murdered her as she was about to catch a taxi. Now Carlo Moro and his henchmen were scouring the town to find and kill Robinson. He didn't know that I was the one whom Vitalia was preparing to join. But he wouldn't spare my life either if he managed to get his hands on me. The Sicilian code was the most summary form of justice in the world.

"I'm sorry, Sinbad… this wasn't supposed to happen…"

We both had to go on the run. This time we took the first boat we could. It was a French-navy ship, *La Marne*, a refuelling tanker. They allowed us to come on board, even though it was against the rules. But Robinson went into great detail about our misfortunes and the danger we were in, owing to the Mafia and Carlo Moro, the scorned husband. That was enough to arouse every French seaman's dormant patriotism. They promised to call at Tripoli, as Robinson wanted to travel through Libya before going home, and then Carthago, where I wanted to nurse my grief, weary of all these sad love affairs. All my hopes in this world ended with Vitalia's death, so Carthago would make a wonderful tomb, a monastery, a huge psychiatric asylum, an open-air prison, and goodness knows what else: the arsehole of the world was perfect for me in my current state of mind. As you know, my lord, this town defies... description...

———

I'D PUT MY THINGS in Major Sied's ship's office. This was a large square room with a panoramic view of the sea and of *La Marne*. The Major was a plump, cheerful man with a splendid moustache. He was second to none when it came to telling jokes. He regarded us provisional seamen as complete rookies, greenhorns.

"The navy has its own language."

And he handed me a dictionary.

"I've noticed you're interested in the written word. A bed is a bunk, a stairway is a ladder. It's easy enough to understand the first expression if you think about what a seaman might miss the most."

He gave me a knowing wink. He sensed I was a man of unfathomable mystery. I was also an explorer of the deep, a swimmer in troubled waters. Anyway, Robinson had more or less put him in the picture about our Sicilian escapade. It explained my gloomy air, my Count of Monte Cristo demeanour, although without the desire for revenge. I really just felt a boundless sadness.

There wasn't much of a female presence on *La Marne*. There were just three women for one hundred and sixty men. On "feminized" ships, explained the Major, nearly a quarter of the crew took the feminine plural, and the showers and toilets were not mixed.

"Showers for women. Whatever next?"

The Major wasn't much of a progressive. He focused mainly on his work on board and the training of young seamen. Most of them had enlisted for the pay, and to see a bit of the world. This meant that when the ship put into port, they would rush over to the postcard-sellers to buy a souvenir to treasure. Some, after the regulation distribution of condoms, would make a beeline for the local prostitutes: doing the rounds of all the brothels and red-light districts on the planet was part of the French navy's mission. I understood those decent men, whose families, thousands of miles away, were quietly waiting for Odysseus's return. There was, when it came down to it, an unspoken rule, and sailors' wives were not unaware of it: a man has needs… and so do women… Back on dry land, men often found their wives hadn't waited for them: they'd run off with a landlubber. Others returned home after several decades at sea and no longer recognized their family. They got fed up, then divorced, then involved with someone else, age permitting. Otherwise, they merely drifted slowly towards the grave.

"It's a tough job," said Monsieur Bouillet, the second-in-command, who was a bit of a philosopher.

The man was a lover of pipes, real pipes made of meer-schaum. In the evening, he would station himself on the bridge, facing out to sea, and smoke his tobacco from the islands. He would spend hours telling me about his voyages, from the Antipodes to the Indian Ocean. Unlike most of his contemporaries, he wasn't overly bothered about the good things in life. His eyes shone with nostalgia for his journeys to foreign parts. He spoke about the land as if it were an unknown woman. An unfamiliar, indistinct woman. He had no

107

family, and all he was interested in was the receding horizon, the storms and the tempests.

A sparrow alighted at the window of Major Sied's ship's office, frail and shivering in the wind battering the deckhouse. It was a long way from land.

"It's vital not to chase it away, otherwise it'll die of exhaustion and drown in the sea," said Major Sied, sensitive to small things.

The Major was lord and master of that ship. Or so he thought. His superior, Commandant Bedaud, a former submariner, didn't share his opinion. The Commandant was a playwright who had penned a play about Pontius Pilate, another famous leader of men. I was allowed to read it because he took a liking to me and thought me possessed of the cardinal virtues of any good critic: hypocrisy and kindness. He was our real lord and master, and he was entitled to preferential treatment. The play, which had never been performed, was about the conscience of a man, Pontius Pilate, whose sentencing was to alter the course of history. The play didn't hang together since it had no dramatic progression and the characters were devoid of any psychological motivation; in short, it entirely lacked a playwright's skill. I was careful not to tell him so, since I didn't want anything to cut short my voyage, which would land me safe and sound in Carthago if I held my tongue.

"Don't say a word, Sinbad, please don't say a word," begged Robinson. "Those weak-willed sailors are slave-traders. You don't know them, you have no idea what lies deep in their souls, which are as unfathomable as the sea."

"They are excellent men."

"I wouldn't stake my life on it. I'm sure they've inherited some fearful practices from their seafaring ancestors."

"Myths, my dear Robinson. Do they eat people in Africa these days?"

"Cannibalism is a scientific fact, Sinbad. A trade-off. A kind of tribute."

And Robinson began humming the popular children's song about how to cook and eat a boy at sea:

> *There was a little ship*
> *That had never sailed*
> *Oh eh, oh eh, mate*
> *Mate, sail onto the sea*

———

S AFETY DRILL on board *La Marne*. The challenge: put out a fire on a boat awash with two types of fuel—F-76 for the ship and F-44 for planes—the main hazard on a ship which in theory never engaged in combat. These endless drills to keep up morale and maintain the physical fitness of the crew and paunchy officers were a real nuisance. The seamen ate well on board, a little too well perhaps; waistlines had a tendency to expand, and then they felt a pressing need to stay on the ball. Thousands of safety drills and countless assorted tricks were put in place to keep their bright-red pompons standing to attention. These ranged from simulated fires to shooting at dummies in the sea—and as no one volunteered to be sniped at, they launched white and red balloons and fired at them, all guns blazing. No one ever hit the targets, so I asked a young officer one day if we would have any chance of surviving an Al Qaeda attack.

"An attack at sea?" asked the young officer.

"Yes."

"It would have to be by pedalo!"

And he began laughing.

"A refuelling tanker isn't equipped to fight off an attack by a Zodiac packed full of explosives."

"What would we do then?"

"We'd pray… that they'd have engine failure, and that there wasn't another Zodiac out there…"

"So what are all these drills for?"

"For Somali pirates… they're very effective against them…"

I slept in the same room as that young officer, who was a virgin. No twenty-year-old man boards a ship with other men unless he lacks sexual experience or is turning his back on life to some extent. What's more, the young officer wanted to bury himself in a nuclear-powered attack submarine. He loved the machine. He dreamt about it on his bunk, the way other men cherish the faraway image of a woman. Not this young officer. He wanted to live in a suppository under the sea with eighty other men, going for months without seeing the sky.

"The missions are sometimes long," the young officer told me.

"How long?"

"Between three and six months on board a submarine. It's magical. Can you imagine? Nuclear propulsion is a technological masterpiece. They miniaturized a nuclear reactor so that it would fit in a submarine. It's perfect. No way of communicating with anyone, for weeks, months…"

"What about your family? Your girlfriend?"

"It's much better not to have a girlfriend, really… but it doesn't bother me… I don't understand women."

"They're not rocket science, you know."

"I don't know… I'm still young. I'd just love to get a posting on a nuclear-powered attack submarine."

"So what floats your boat is something like the Sistine Chapel of weaponry?"

"Never seen the Sistine Chapel. Is it in Rome?"

110

In the engine room, the house of the dead, a noisy Hades, I met two of the other women on the boat, Tabatha and Samantha. The two engines had been so christened by the stokers who continually burned and inhaled diesel. You had to wear a noise-reduction helmet to descend into the belly of the whale. Behind a fire door, five or six seamen were sitting at security monitors in a stiflingly hot green room. There was the stink of burning diesel and you could lose pints of water in there. You had to keep rehydrating yourself.

"You get used to the smell and the heat," one of the mechanics told me. "I don't notice it any more."

Later, another man confided that he'd also like to work on board a nuclear-powered submarine, so it was a common dream in the navy. Perhaps it was the poetry of the depths, or the appeal of technology due to an increase in video war games. I had no idea why they all wanted to be cooped up together in a metal cigar. You had to have no confidence in the future, to reject the world with all your might, with all the strength of a condemned man. Maybe those youngsters longed for the grave because they were deeply aware of the finite nature of things. I didn't know, even though I understood their desire for a premature end, but I was much older than they were. I was clearly getting sentimental.

This prospective candidate for the emptiness of the deep was of Turkish descent, so there was a danger that he might not be accepted for the training programme. They didn't trust second-generation French seamen. Besides, few of them fitted in, being snubbed by the other seamen, who were racist. This man had quite a mouth on him, so the other men treated him with respect. Some of them preferred to hand in their resignation while others put up with it. But nothing prevented this youngster, this Captain Nemo in the making, from dreaming of the deep. Had he read *Twenty Thousand Leagues Under the Sea*? No. He wasn't much of a reader. He didn't have time on board *La Marne*... Do you need time to read? Yes, of course. So where did he get this vague dream from? He was fascinated by technology, engines and machines, and by far the sexiest of them all was powered by atomic energy; it was machine royalty, man's mechanical future, the power of fire harnessed in a box by man as machine. Jules Verne would have felt at home with these men.

MAJOR SIED pulled on a tool belt and made for the laundry, where he would kit out his men with thick fireproof clothes and oxygen cylinders. The drill would last half an hour. After that, the seamen would train with pump-action rifles. As Commandant Bedaud explained, *La Marne* was lightly armed for defence purposes. He had previously served on a submarine before ending up on a refuelling tanker: a massive vessel which was more like a floating fridge than a frigate. In the Commandant's view, the tanker had nothing on the submarine, which was a marvel.

You soon became burnt out on a submarine, though. One day, the doc would summon you to his office and tell you it was time to return to the surface. It was never a big drama. But when they came back up, the men weren't really men any more. They'd lost all contact with the real world, provided that it really exists in the first place, philosophized the Commandant. They had no friends, no wives, no children... they had to rebuild their lives at the age of thirty-five. Impossible. The will wasn't there any more. It was a bit like asking a monk to leave his order. Or telling Christ to get down from his cross. There was no doubt the Commandant knew his history, since he'd written a play about Pontius Pilate.

"The Libyans want us to fly a courtesy flag."

"And is that a problem, Commandant?"

"It goes against all the laws of navigation. Every single one. I will refer this to a higher authority. I can't make this decision on my own. We're not going to disembark if it means backing down. Out of the question!"

Naturally, when we disembarked, we were flying the Libyan flag.

In Tripoli, after we had landed on the shores of the Gulf of Sirte, Robinson and I prepared to say our farewells.

"Well, mate, I'm heading home; through the vast desert expanses."

"That's the road to Medina!"

"Stop lecturing me, Sinbad. Haven't you got anything better to do than show off your cultural knowledge to a barbarian like me?"

"Culture is you, Robinson!"

"I'm sorry, Sinbad... about Vitalia..."

I think I wept then, like a child, overcome with sadness. Robinson put his arms around me and began singing a Negro lullaby. I didn't understand many of the words, but it warmed my cold heart.

We were walking through old Tripoli in the sunshine. The country seemed to be laying itself open. A sign on the wall of the citadel announced in Arabic: "We are happy to live in the time of the supreme leader." There were still some fine times ahead of the Cyclops. Robinson took his leave and headed off into Tripoli's narrow streets. I lost sight of him near a stall where a coppersmith was working at his craft: one of the town's many attractions, a scene which could have been lifted from one of the *Corto Maltese* comics. The light was gentle, like an old acquaintance, and blue as an orange. I stopped near an ancient tenth-century minaret. It looked like a lighthouse. The song of the muezzin trickled out through the loopholes. I thought it was probably prayer time. I entered the mosque and knelt on the carpet. My soul was empty and my words had no meaning. They bubbled up like a wild song in the dim light. I swallowed my sorrow and my tears. I drank them. They were bitter and I vomited them onto the carpet, surrounded by the night music of the soul. I vomited this world like a sailor after a drunken night on the town.

XI

AFTER MY LIBYAN EPISODE, I had gone back to Carthago and had immediately been thrown into jail and put on a diet of dry bread and water.

What was I accused of?

Poisoning Carthago's president for life, Chafouin I. According to some well-informed sources, a meal of couscous wolfed down one evening with a few soldiers from a rival clan had caused this tragedy, which was—quite wrongly—laid at my door.

When Chafouin I, president for life, had swallowed his last chickpea, he began suffering horrific spasms and fiendish pains. He then brought up the couscous, the meatballs and sundry rotten vegetables, along with part of his stomach. At the sight of this visceral avalanche, they shoved him, covered with blood and vomit, onto a private jet which took him to France, and the Val-de-Grâce hospital in Paris, straight into the lion's jaws, really, if you consider that Chafouin I had been inveighing against the former colonial power only the evening before, asking the international authorities to impose sanctions on the fucking French who'd tortured Algerians as well as independent, popular Algeria, something that Chafouin I, King of the North African Belgians, refused to condone.

While I was in jail, I had time to miss Vitalia and sweet Giovanna. I remembered the former's voluptuous curves and her skin sweet as fruit, our reunion in Sicily, and our eternal love sanctified by death; when I remembered the latter, I recalled the image of a woman as hot as summer days. Anyway, I had been receiving passionate letters from her since she'd somehow tracked me down, although I'm not sure how. I would learn later that my disappearance had created quite a stir in Rome. Giovanna, as militant as they come, just the way I like my women, spread the news through the Eternal City, *Urbi et Orbi*, and even appealed to Pope Ratzinger, who sanctimoniously informed her that he couldn't give a damn about the fate of one Mohammedan, who was just as quarrelsome as the rest of his race. To back up his words and by way of a reply to the beautiful Giovanna, who'd jeopardized her reputation by consorting with the Infidel, he produced a kind of papal bull in which he implied, by means of a completely invented dialogue which was supposed to have taken place in the thirteenth century, that the sons of Islam were arrant rogues and foul murderers.

"Show me just what Mohammed brought that was new and there you will find things only bad and inhuman, such as his command to spread by the sword the faith he preached," added Benedict XVI, quoting, for Giovanna's benefit, a sentence from a fourteenth-century dialogue in which a Byzantine emperor is addressing a "cultivated Persian".

There were even a few Muslim intellectuals who praised the Immobile Pope's broad theoretical vision and felt he was voicing a sound criticism of the deadliest religion in humanity, which was theirs only by chance. The beautiful and very wise Giovanna told the Holy Roman Church that, even in the thirteenth century, peace-loving Christians had burnt the Albigensians at the stake, and that during the Crusades in Syria, at Maarat, the home town of the famous poet Abul Ala Al-Ma'arri, they had carved and eaten Infidels at a great feast, which would have horrified Christ.

The Sinbad Affair, which was now going global, wasn't helped by the fact that Turkish fanatics raped the last three nuns left on the Anatolian plateau and slit the throats of two Orthodox priests, who hadn't digested the papal bull. During this period, Bush's Americans invaded and destroyed Iraq, scattering several thousand years of history and looting the national museum in Baghdad which had housed the treasures of Mesopotamia. They burnt the early manuscripts of the Qur'an and decimated the circular town, exactly as the Mongols had done in bygone days, followed by Basra, the port where Sinbad used to drop anchor when he returned from each of his voyages and which was, from then on, as English as in the good old days of the British Empire on which the sun never sets. I should make it clear that I'm referring to the real Sinbad here, the man of legend, not the poor prisoner who, despite a worldwide campaign, had been rotting in the presidential jail for several months. But Giovanna hadn't had her final say: she threatened Paduzzi di Balto that she would go public about their private life, since she'd barely reached the age of consent when their affair started, if he did nothing to help one of the Villa Medici's former residents. Paduzzi knew a lot of people in Paris. He obtained the help of Jacques Chirac, who insisted that his great friend President Chafouin I, whose pitiful illness had been treated at the Val-de-Grâce military hospital, should set free the most inoffensive political prisoner in the world. The latter granted his request on condition that he in turn would give Sinbad asylum in France. He didn't want someone like Sinbad in Carthago any more, whether he was a patriotic nationalist or not.

So I arrived in Paris to be greeted by a cheering crowd. Giovanna, who was waiting for me at the airport, proposed to me after suffocating me in her arms for far too long and showering me with tears of happiness. I'd only just escaped from captivity, and I wasn't about to return to it; still stunned by the crowd's jubilation and the size of the welcoming committee at Charles de Gaulle airport, who were celebrating my arrival as though I were the Messiah, I refused the bonds of marriage which I felt were more terrifying than the smallest dungeon. In a fit of pique, Giovanna returned to Rome where, rumour has it, she's enjoying a good life with her one true love, Paduzzi di Balto.

———

I WAS DAZZLED by Paris, the City of Light, a name I'd shout out loud while strolling along its boulevards or walking by the Seine, remembering Apollinaire. At Père Lachaise cemetery, I bowed down before Balzac's tomb. If I hadn't held myself back for fear of being mocked by the girls laying flowers on the grave of that drunkard Jim Morrison, I'd probably have exclaimed, like my cult hero, Rastignac: "It's between the two of us now!"

Since it's never too late to get an education, I enrolled at the Sorbonne, where I was intending to read classics. At the university, I wasn't disappointed: I was the only man in my year and all the other students were women who were certainly not backward in coming forward. I lost no time in inviting them to my room at 35 Boulevard du Montparnasse, a stone's throw from Rue Campagne-Première, where Elsa Triolet and Louis Aragon had conducted their secret love affair. My landlady, France, was very fond of me, even if she did scold me gently for the trail of broken hearts I left in my wake.

France was an attractive woman in her forties, who'd left her husband, Monsieur Tschann, to run off with a Malian poet called Hérode, whom I disliked intensely. He regarded himself as the spiritual son of Léopold Sédar Senghor, the great grammarian before God and, besides that, one of the poets who had created the *Négritude* movement, which had been enjoying a new lease of life since his death. As I preferred Aimé Césaire, who was more sincere, I decided that Hérode, France's belligerent lover, was my sworn enemy. Hérode had published just two pamphlets and he already thought he was Ronsard, Du Bellay and the other members of the Pléiade rolled into one. He went around declaring that no one had produced better poetry since Boileau.

Naturally, he adored Céline—he would read him aloud to France at night before bed—and was very proud of loving *A La Recherche*. He had also turned his hand to writing novels so that he might be ranked with Proust. After ten years of hard work, during which time he'd weighed each word the way a grocer weighs butter, chopped up his sentences the way a butcher chops cutlets, and bored France rigid with the migraines and bellyaches of a great writer, he finally succeeded in publishing a short novel called *Le Bouton d'Anaïs*: a metaphor for the war in Angola, seen through the eyes of a young, streetwise girl who prostituted herself to the soldiers of both camps. However, since Hérode had come up with the bright idea of making the girl talk like someone from the Guermantes family, the book was very funny.

No one told him that it was, of course, especially France, blinded by love for her great prose writer.

When he wasn't cheating on France with primary-school teachers who shared his weakness for school-book French, Hérode would launch into cruel diatribes against all African writers who, he thought, spoke and wrote French *perfectly*. He'd place great emphasis on this adverb, rolling it around his mouth, opening his mocking eyes very wide, his lips pursed to roll the "r"s *perfectly*, showing his scorn for the little nigger of their ancestors. He'd been raised by the white fathers who'd instilled in him a love for his fellow man and the cadenced language of the Bible, while those *shitty* little scribblers would never be free of the chip on their shoulders that came from *growing up* in a colonized country bathed in the sun of independence; those piccaninnies had never seen a Vermeer, knew nothing about Monet (*let alone Manet!*), didn't

119

understand Picasso, had never even heard of Kandinsky and would never die like Bergotte in front of the little patch of yellow wall in Delft. What's more, they were still idolaters, terrifying animists who pierced their nostrils, Jesuit-devouring cannibals, wild animals who voted by striking their paunches to the rhythm of the tom-tom, incestuous men who raped nuns at the slightest sign of revolt and hacked poor Tutsis to pieces with machetes, lechers who had their daughters circumcised, then sold them, and alkies who never smashed their glasses. He, on the other hand, drank his lime-blossom infusion or, occasionally, a little red wine to treat his ulcer, while reading *L'après-midi d'un Faune* and listening to the *Gymnopédies*.

The only time he was a Negro was when he had to renew his residence papers at the police headquarters in Paris, where being Malian was essential as far as the cops were concerned and was even more important than his knowledge of French and all its subtleties. On that day, amidst all those anxious strangers with their hangdog expressions—I too had to submit to that humiliating ritual—he became the Negro he'd never ceased to be and I became the Arab with a knife gripped between my teeth.

One day, I told Hérode about my admiration for the author of the *New Voyages of Sinbad*.

"Hear that, France? Your young protégé… that writer…"

Like a comic-opera Othello, Hérode was beside himself with jealousy if any young man went near France.

"He lived here for a year," recalled France with a hint of nostalgia that infuriated Hérode.

"Lived, lived, that's a bit of an overstatement! He was a snail, a hack! It's a wonder he managed to write that novel at all."

"He was talented, my darling."

Hérode glared at her.

"Much less talented than you, darling, of course. No doubt about that."

"Those Arabs"—you could tell the word had a capital letter!—"those Arabs can't write. I tried to read his book: a complete dud in my opinion. It gave me such a headache. Too many sentences, too many words. You see, my dear Sinbad, the French language can't tolerate overindulgence. It has a delicate stomach."

He gave a loud laugh. Then he fell silent, rubbing his stomach with a grimace.

"His ulcer is hurting," said France. "Poor darling. Would you like a glass of milk, my love?"

"Milk! Always milk! Do you think literature can tolerate milk!"

"What about Proust, darling, remember Proust. He drank a lot of milk."

"You're right. A small glass won't do me any harm."

France handed him his drink and he immersed his little round, black lips in it. They were white now and made him look like a child who'd smeared his face with chocolate at teatime. I couldn't be annoyed with Hérode, I just thought he was juvenile and given to extremes of behaviour, like a child beaten by his parents at home, who begins striking his schoolmates in the playground.

In Paris, I strolled along the Boulevard Montparnasse, lost myself in Rue de la Gaîté, and sat at a table on Place Quinet, musing on Pascin surrounded by his prostitutes, Picasso, rich and famous but still in love, all those radiant passers-by who'd filled the streets and cafés of this area, which still had its charms and yet was facing its demise.

I was appalled by death, which seemed like a lousy end to life's slow dying. I didn't understand the philosophers who denied death or poured scorn on it. I was a medieval man. I much preferred the *danse macabre* of plague-sufferers and witches to our modern-day denial, to the hospitals—those huge, cold, clean residences where the condemned were dumped out of sight and mind, like the old men and women who died alone in dingy apartments, things put away in a cupboard and forgotten. Death didn't exist for my agile contemporaries, those little starlets who hurried up and down the Boulevard du Montparnasse, bought their cigarettes at Le Brazza at two o'clock in the morning or got drunk in La Coupole, that cold, impersonal tourist trap of a café-bar. Death had deserted the Rue Notre-Dame-des-Champs, where poor Rilke had walked with his creation, the terrible and solitary Malte Laurids Brigge:

"Did I say it before? I'm learning to see—yes, I'm making a start. I'm still not good at it. But I want to make the most of my time.

"For example, I've never actually wondered how many faces there are. There are a great many people, but there are even more faces because each person has several. There are those who wear one face for years on end; naturally, it starts to wear, it gets dirty, it breaks at the folds, it becomes stretched like gloves that are kept for travelling. These are thrifty, simple people; they don't change their faces, and never for once would they have them cleaned. It's good enough, they maintain, and who can convince them otherwise? Admittedly, since they have several faces, the question now arises: what do they do with the others? They save them. They'll do for the children. There have even been instances when dogs have gone out with them on. And why not? A face is a face.

"Other people change their faces one after the other with uncanny speed and wear them out. At first it seems to them that they've enough to last them for ever, but before they're even forty they're down to the last of them. Of course, there's a tragic side to it. They're not used to looking after faces; their last one wore through in a week and has holes in it, and in many places it's as thin as paper; bit by bit the bottom layer, the non-face, shows through and they go about wearing that.

"But that woman, that woman: bent forward with her head in her hands, she'd completely fallen into herself. It was at the corner

122

of Rue Notre-Dame-des-Champs. I began to tread softly the moment I caught sight of her. Poor people shouldn't be disturbed when they're deep in thought. What they're searching for might still occur to them.

"The street was too empty; its emptiness was bored with itself and it pulled away the sounds of my footsteps and clattered around all over the place with them like a wooden clog. Out of fright the woman reared up too quickly, too violently, so that her face was left in her two hands. I could see it lying there, the hollowness of its shape. It cost me an indescribable effort to keep looking at those hands and not at what they'd torn away from. I dreaded seeing the inside of a face, but I was much more afraid of the exposed rawness of the head without a face."

———

I WAS WORKING on a modern literature PhD about Casanova at the Sorbonne. I supplemented my hours of study with practical research carried out with the help of fellow students, who were chosen for their long hair, ample bust and slim legs. My first victim was a slender schooner called Caline, who had a mane full of Venetian-red highlights.

I'd learnt from reading *The Memoirs of Casanova* that young women in the lagoon city covered their hair with a mixture of saffron and lemon, then dried it on the terraces of the *palazzi* in summer to obtain this particular colour. Caline had no need of such methods to suffuse her face with light. When she undressed, a quick look down below confirmed that the truth is often hidden from plain sight. So, as a fascinated disciple of Mesmer, another illustrious character from that sublime century, I moved closer to that stomach, full and round as the sun, and kissed it with burning lips and a penetrating tongue.

And Caline, who wasn't shy—her dissertation was on the eighteenth-century libertine writers—spread her thighs so that I could explore all the subtleties therein. Being an assiduous researcher, I pored over her sex to extract its very substance. I parted pretty Caline's lips with the delicate touch of a butterfly-collector extracting the lepidopteran from his net. My fingers were gently spreading the brightly coloured wings of the lovely insect I was about to devour, when Caline shut her elytra against me and turned over to show me her buttocks. No one could find fault with that; she had such perfect, round, firm buttocks that the mere sight made a poor student like myself lose control: my proboscis lengthened and knocked against that arse, then entered via the dark line splitting that miracle of nature into two globes, while Caline, an amorous nymph searching for her imago, pressed back against my cock.

Caline wasn't a screamer. When I disappeared between her thighs, a ship sucked in by that maelstrom, she didn't make the slightest murmur, she just fluttered her wings like a belladonna or amaryllis flower, and the skin of her face turned the colour of her hair, her gaze blurred and her eyes rolled up before closing as she flowed, liquid and dreamy between my fingers: Ophelia floating on the water in her white veils.

Caline was flighty, just like the butterflies, and I didn't manage to capture her often; despite lying in wait for her when she came out of lectures, she evaded me, as evanescent as a soul, shifting like those flames adored by the Persians, which divided the world into darkness and light. I put up with my lover's changes of mood and let her go with good grace. I consoled myself with another woman, whom I met in the university cafeteria, and who was the polar opposite of Caline.

Mazarine was preparing to take the teachers' certificate in philosophy and looked like Shakespeare's dark lady. Another man might have said she was bad news and would have run a mile. She dressed all in black and would lose herself in endless dark reveries that would suck me down and destroy my proverbial good mood. Mazarine looked something like one of the Divine Marquis's heroines. She was a philosopher imprisoned in her boudoir. Mazarine spent her time pondering on being and nothingness, taking roads leading nowhere, and dividing herself between being and time; that is, when she wasn't discussing ethics with Nicomaque, her classmate. Nicomaque was fond of Spinoza and was wondering whether he shouldn't soon join Toni Negri, now in prison, in order to support the armed conflict begun in Italy two decades earlier.

Mazarine and Nicomaque, who thought I was a political simpleton and a philosophical jerk, believed that the Republic had been superseded since the death of Socrates and no recourse to method would reinstate it. Even *Das Kapital*, armed with its will to power, was, beyond considerations of good and evil, powerless to bring back the ancient liberal heresy and the illusion of democracy. Purely to annoy those morons, I would launch into a defence of Socrates, then invite them to a banquet in one of those revolting little restaurants in the Latin Quarter, where you could drink as much wine as you liked, on Rue Monsieur-le-Prince, for example, or somewhere between the Rue de la Harpe and the Boulevard Saint-Michel, now entirely given over to second-hand-clothes shops and hordes of American girls looking for adventure in the oldest and most authentic quarter of Paris. It goes without saying that my invitation to travel was usually ignored on the pretext of urgently having to read the *Tractatus Logico-Philosophicus*, which I confused with the ficus of my childhood, which grew on the Cours de la Révolution in Carthago and which, instead of enlightening my mind, provided me with shade in the scorching midsummer heat.

When evening came, Nicomaque went back to sleep in his tub and I was left alone with Mazarine in a room that Pascal would have liked, before falling asleep between two harrowing infinities.

125

As a hedonist, some might say a cynic, I pounced on Mazarine because it has long been known that man is a wolf to woman, and women are the future of men, when they lie down on a bed and accommodate the seed that never dies in their womb.

A dedicated reader of the *Diary of a Seducer* and the *120 Jours de Sodome*, I found I was armed with the necessary, contingent concepts to appeal to Mazarine, who was more like Justine than the Princess of Cleves when it came to what she liked in bed. Mazarine never took off her clothes, you had to rip off her dress, her bra, her black lace knickers, and tear off stockings held up by an ingenious system. Mazarine liked to be bound and treated roughly by her lover who, fascinated once more by this new experience, let himself be guided by his mistress's unbridled imagination as she invented obscene storylines, scenes in which he played the lead, often an oriental potentate dressed as a caliph from the *Arabian Nights* or a lascivious sheikh straight out of a Tintin comic book.

The Bashi-Bazouk captured the innocent Mazarine, threw her down onto the floor and dragged her by the hair onto a carpet that she'd spread out beforehand. I then ripped off her clothes as she fought back wildly, kicking out in all directions, which put my back out and left me black and blue.

When Mazarine was naked, I skilfully tied her up and suspended her from the ceiling. I became a master of knots and knew all the tricks of the trade; one day, my expertise even earned me an invitation to Japan. I stayed in one of those fine wood-and-paper houses which were designed to withstand earthquakes, tsunamis and other disasters, and had high, sturdy rafters from which young women with coal-black manes could be hung like lanterns.

In the meantime, insatiable, crazy Mazarine screamed and raved, and spat at the poor leather-clad wretch wielding a ridiculous cat-o'-nine-tails, trying to quieten her before the police showed up and arrested this Indiana Jones for assault, gross indecency, breach of the peace at night, false imprisonment and acts of barbarism.

So with a heavy heart, I gave Mazarine a good spanking, which calmed her down. She wept a few tears before untying herself and subjecting me to the worst-imaginable indignities in retaliation. These erotic devices, which equalled anything in De Sade—I employed his hilarious methods every evening—eventually wore me out. I missed lovely Caline and her more temperate ways.

So you can imagine my relief when Mazarine went to Italy with Nicomaque to join the Red Brigades, or what was left of them, scattered here and there in transalpine prisons.

———

CRINOLINE'S MANE OF HAIR was almost red. She was luscious as a watermelon, with a beautiful face and rare, almost superhuman sex appeal. Men's eyes lit up like Chinese lanterns when she walked down the street. She could have been mistaken for Norma Jean, not so much Marilyn, although she moved in the same fluid way, sashaying like a flame about to be blown out. Like the Californian bombshell, Crinoline dreamt of setting the world on fire as an actress after causing a couple of dozen hearts to self-combust. She'd worked in a drama school, but had never been paid a fee; still, she had fingered the purses of every man in the troupe, from the extras to the director, Yannis Karski, who was a fan of the theatre of cruelty.

His actors performed naked and experimented with strange choreographies. You could be sceptical at the sight of those well-fed young women and men piled on top of each other to simulate the death camps. According to Yannis Karski, their performances in Avignon had been even more awe-inspiring. That had been on the fringe circuit, of course, murmured the director, who organized free workshops that entailed taking his students for long rambles in the woods. The aim of these exercises was survival in a hostile

127

environment. Without provisions or a compass, the apprentice actors had to find their way back after camping out for several days in very overcrowded conditions. Naturally, repeated Yannis Karski, they had to throw all their inhibitions to the wind and abandon all bourgeois notions of morality.

Crinoline was proud that she had passed through the great Yannis's hands. He'd opened up new horizons for her, and had moulded her after the crucial step of taking her as his mistress.

"Yannis has gone beyond Aristotelian theatre. He has challenged five thousand years of tradition. No more mimesis! We were totally in the Noh! We danced, drank, and fucked under the stars. You wouldn't understand. We suffered too. A lot."

With Yannis Karski's help, Crinoline had become a mediocre actress, except in bed, where she turned into a lioness and devoured me, screaming noisily. Crinoline was a pleasure-seeker with the voice of a bald prima donna in rude health. She would straddle me for hours while sounding the alarm, engulfing me so entirely that I forgot the world, my ears filled with her roaring orgasms, my prick and balls were drenched. As well as being a songbird, Crinoline was a one-woman fountain. The first time, I was taken aback when I was showered by the forceful stream she projected. I was sure she'd pissed on me.

That wasn't the case at all, explained the young woman, who produced copious amounts of a liquid that was as colourless and odourless as eau-de-vie. Crinoline was a little ashamed at spilling herself like this. I tried the liqueur that Crinoline distilled, but it didn't taste of anything. Crinoline was right. It was a mysterious product which no one had thought to patent. It was a shame. Liquid women like Crinoline were on the verge of extinction, so they had to be protected like the panda, polar bear or blue whale. There were renowned scientists who thought that these women drenched their victims as they climaxed in order to dampen their ardour. Snapping your banjo string was a real danger with those vixens who came onto you like amazons, turned you on like little dynamos and pressed your valves as if you were a trumpet in a free-jazz solo. In their own way, they were sparing their rides by splashing them with water to cool them down.

Other engineers in female mechanics claimed that these women simply pissed on their lovers to satisfy some obscure fantasy. A hypothesis called into question by my knowledge of liquids, which was as bottomless as the ocean, since I'd personally sampled all the cunts in creation, particularly Giovanna's, and she was a woman who loved her water sports.

I didn't deny there was something comical about the tsunamis orchestrated by Crinoline. And yet my desire increased tenfold and my cock grew even longer because of them. I lost my memory between Crinoline's thighs as she raced over me like a locomotive, making me blow my whistle for minutes on end. But, one day, Crinoline left me. Yannis Karski had returned and wanted her back in his troupe. She took French leave, slipping away like the water between her legs. I missed her a little, but not that much.

It didn't take long to replace her: a plump professor at the Sorbonne; a few nurses picked up at the Salpêtrière Hospital one day when I had a problem of an intimate nature that led me to consult an eminent urologist, Professor Fawcett, who declared me fit for service and introduced me to his entire team, as well as his wife, who was only too happy to finish the consultation that her husband had started; two student nurses sunbathing in the Jardin du Luxembourg, whom I fondled behind the Medici Fountain; my neighbour at 35 Boulevard du Montparnasse, who was unfortunate enough to ask me for a knob of butter and who lost her virginity while dancing her last tango in Paris on the bedroom floor; the cleaning lady who was young and pretty and who looked nothing like the horrible Madame Pinto she occasionally replaced; a racist Portuguese woman; and an Egyptian opera singer I met in the Parc Monceau—she lived in the apartment block opposite and practised scales fit to deafen her neighbours, who called her a North African cow and a Maghrebi bitch, causing her to seek consolation in my arms. Then there was the baker's wife who lovingly kneaded and baked my baguette; the cashier from the Franprix supermarket in Rue Vavin, whose glasses drove me wild because removing them excited me more than unzipping her dresses between the cartons of Candia milk, Nestlé chocolate and plain or fruit Yoplait yoghurt; and the RATP driver who came to my aid when I was attacked by two skinheads on a Metro train and whose light green uniform, which cinched in her breasts and waist, was, in my opinion, a sensual triumph and by far my most favourite thing. There was also the only female taxi driver I ever met who didn't look like a man and who listened to *The Four Seasons*, which led us to improvise a Baroque recital in the Class C Mercedes she'd parked in the middle of the Bois de Boulogne, while strange onlookers gathered to watch and listen to the concert. Not to mention the female passers-by described by Baudelaire, the girls of Paris, the cheeky skirts on the Pont des Arts lifted by the wind, love at twenty, the young girls painted by Pascin; and a reincarnation, at the exact age she was when she met Picasso, of Marie-Thérèse, whom I left for fear of ending up in jail again—I wasn't a famous painter and moral standards had changed a great deal in a century; and the girls from the Bateau-Lavoir, Place Émile-Goudeau, who were reading the engraved bronze plaque that said that various famous painters had lived, worked and loved in this square: Modigliani committed suicide, Chagall played violin on a roof, Soutine flayed animals which, in his lifetime, frightened the burghers of Calais, whose company I never sought out, being so afraid of the greed and stupidity criticized by Flaubert; and the women of Montparnasse between the Rue Campagne-Première and the Rue de la Gaîté where, one evening, I had greedily kissed a young Italian tourist and taken her to a hotel room on the Rue Delambre to worship her stomach, legs and buttocks; and finally, one night at the far end of the Île Saint-Louis, another willing stray, whom I covered with my voluminous black coat, then caressed and penetrated, while the *bateaux-mouches* illuminated us and the tourists cheered because Paris is the town of lovers, Paris is a celebration and Paris will always be Paris for those who love each other everywhere, on the banks of the Seine, beneath the porches, and in the streets, like cats and dogs.

XII

THE SORBONNE. The Cour d'honneur. The building dated from the nineteenth century and provided a setting for the seventeenth-century chapel built by Richelieu, a rare example of classical architecture in Paris. This was where that wretched highway robber was buried, then exhumed by sans-culottes, who dismembered the body and threw it to the jubilant crowd. The skull was eventually retrieved, in two pieces, during Victor Hugo's century, and replaced in the chapel where it was sealed in concrete. The cardinal had a hard head and a quick hand when it came to fleecing the Parisians with crushing taxes. The people of Paris, before they disappeared in the late fifties to be replaced by a bleating herd motivated only by childish nonsense, were vulgar, tumultuous, free and resentful. The women were strumpets and nags, who hadn't yet begun to regard themselves as Belle Époque courtesans. And, more than a century after the Cardinal's death, a few stout-hearted fellows, whose great-grandfathers had died crippled by debt, unleashed their fury on his wretched sepulchre in the name of revenge.

I was waiting for Caline again, and again she was late. A young student was sitting next to me, her things—a bag, various papers and a CD—were spread out on the stone bench on which we were sitting. She looked anxious. And yet she was talking nineteen to the dozen, trying to fill the empty spaces in her head. She was chatting to her friend. A scruffy young man, looking trendy in Levi's jeans and jacket. They were talking about Nietzsche, and Plato. Nothing they said was worth repeating. An exchange of platitudes, scraps from their lectures, clichés gleaned from books. We live in such ignorant times!

Tourists walk by in single file. Some of the sheep are interested in the chapel, the others in the sundial which is supposed to tell the time. When, I wonder, will they ban mandatory package holidays? Will we have to wait for a global epidemic or a viral plague to force nations to ban flights, travel from the Antipodes, Teutonic charters, Tunisian beaches, the Vatican, Mecca? A new religion will soon be born that will proclaim the reign of Intelligence and Pleasure, and I shall be its Prophet.

Words overheard. Sun. Awesome. *Richeliou.*

How has this light-filled city, one of the wonders of Europe, where people always used to value the spirit rather than the letter of the law, become so benighted? I asked myself: how was it that, in barely fifty years, the talent that used to spring up from under the trollops' feet, like weeds between the cracks of the pavement, had disappeared beneath the dog shit? All that remained was the stupidity that Flaubert had feared so much. And it had spread—it attacked the poor, the foreigner with no money to defend himself, and it massacred the Sinbads of the world, with their noses pressed up against the windows of that empty store filled with millions of naked, soulless mannequins operated by an absurd mechanism that allowed them to get up in the morning, drink their coffee while tetchily spouting crap gleaned from the newspaper or television, then leave home to triumph over a bleak day in which the workplace provided an excuse for waging war against their fellow man, particularly if he showed any talent. People respected money, the arrogance that came with money, and the wielders of briefcases who'd been in power for the past two decades. Farewell to the teeming brood, the republican trollops, the glorious artists and the little cafés.

I looked at the young philosopher, I sensed I was her unlucky star, the dark planet interfering with her concentration. She pulled her bags, papers and CD closer.

The tourists unsheath their cameras: unimportant, unsightly contraptions, most of them with defective lenses. They are ready to start their digital shooting. Bang. Bang. Death to the lovely seventeenth-century chapel. Death to the sundial which they don't like. Death to the students in meaningless images taken by weekend photographers. Death to Doisneau, Man Ray, Evans. Death to the sunless day.

I caught myself hoping that somewhere a little fragment of eternity had slipped into the camera held by one of the crowd. A furtive kiss. A student picking his nose.

I remembered a photo taken in Carthago.

A little girl going to school, carrying a schoolbag bigger than her. She was peacefully making her way to school. Behind her, two soldiers were carrying Kalashnikovs slung across their shoulders. Behind the soldiers, graffiti on the wall: "Vive le FIS". The photographer had summed up an entire tragic decade. Childhood threatened by hordes of fanatical killers, and soldiers who were just as bad. Carthago had died in those bloody years. Clearly, it would never recover from those terrible massacres; no Sleeper and his dog could change that.

I remembered the little girl's innocence as she made her way to school, dwarfed by her schoolbag. Could a child save the world? It was a serious question that might amuse fools, but serious none the less, I was certain of it. I couldn't see any children left on this earth, all I could see were terrible, powerful adults of all ages, a sort of village of the damned. Innocence, if it had ever existed, had died in the space of a quarter of a century, and I, Sinbad, noticed its absence every day when some poor wretch and his family were chased off because their skin wasn't the right colour, every day when a bomb set fire to a village somewhere in the world because of obscure oil interests, consolidating the position of a puppet potentate in full possession of nothing. I wasn't so naive as to think we had souls—we, the damned of this earth, the once colonized peoples who had come through every kind of disaster. Even the sons of the Shoah were respectable executioners now; we were decent cannibals who rutted grotesquely then gave birth to hideous offspring.

Watching the tourists put their weapons away, I wondered if the little girl in the photo was still alive. To tell the truth, I didn't hope for it too strongly. I was afraid of that girl as an adult, afraid that she'd probably been press-ganged into the world I was trying to escape, a perpetual exile, a horrified witness of the air-conditioned nightmare.

If there's one thing I hope for in this world, it's that she's still alive, as intact as a piece of porcelain.

The tourists consult each other noisily about the direction they should take. Those with less of a herd instinct start to head for the exit.

The young student gathers up her things, puts them in her bag, then puts her bag to one side.

I despise her for thinking I might want to steal her bag.

Elevated Metro station. Dupleix. Grey sky. It's cold and humid as usual in Paris: the prevailing colour is bronze, a bronze, Platonic town, but nothing to do with the age of the same name. This is a prosaic era which regards plastic as a noble material. Some idiots are advocating a return to the soil, the whole shebang, that god-awful glorification of the country yokel which has even the most hard-line Parisian daydreaming about Mother Earth. It's the hopelessly entrenched side of the only nation in the world so devoted to their mangrove swamps.

Why not simply wait for death, a return to generative sources? When the people of this country return to the earth, become one with it, fertilize it and nourish it with maggots, they prefer to be shut inside boxes that will stand the test of time, or they want to be cremated so they can end up on the mantelpiece. This is the only place on earth where the population's main concern in the morning, like a constipated man holding out little hope when he tries to have a bowel movement, is gazing at its reflection in the mirror. "Am I fair, O mortals?" asks the old lady in a wig. You can't open a newspaper, read an article or watch a television programme without people talking, debating and arguing about what France is: France, France, France... ad nauseam... But France means nothing now, that's why people are trying to find it... it's an old idea that's dead and gone, swept under a carpet by a cleaning lady, a Muslim in a burqa, for example, or an African polygamist, a scumbag from the Paris suburbs or a Carthaginian in exile.

France is the early-morning street-sweepers, the men who pick up the shit of the little dogs walked by the old dears, the unseen workers, the Bengali kitchen-hands no one ever notices, who fill the Metro with the fragrance of garlic and spices in the evenings when they are so tired that they fall off their seats; it is the Algerians hated for daring to emerge from colonial darkness, whose children are living remorse for this crime, the Vietnamese and Chinese crammed into the unluckily numbered thirteenth *arrondissement*, who have become so much part of the scenery that no one notices them any more. This is the fragrant, invisible country, the country that people would rather do without, even at the risk of disappearing, body and soul, and ending up like Switzerland: France's alternative destiny, a country filled with cuckoo clocks and bankers, an earthly paradise for cows and Nazis.

137

I'd just missed a train, so I sat down. There are other passengers waiting. No two look alike. The Metro is the only place where you're sure to see the whole range of humanity. An elderly black man is pacing up and down the station. He's wearing a threadbare coat and is carefully examining the steel superstructures supporting and elevating the station. The sun detonates against the glass of the windows, slides between the metal girders and bounces off the rails where a boy is trying to perform some acrobatic moves. One of the travellers calls out to him. He climbs back onto the platform, proud of his feat. The elderly black man is still pacing up and down the station, contemplating the marriage of steel and metal, force and permanence. He is enraptured by this masterpiece of ingenuity and engineering.

A man sits down next to me. I have the vague impression that I've seen him before. I look a lot like him. He could be my brother. Robinson?

The Book of Stations. The Great Book of Stations. Think about all you can learn from consulting the Metro map.

Who's speaking?

Me or him?

The solo voice continues in the dazzling light. Every station has its own history, its own spaces. Endless species. You can travel through time, straddle the entire Russian Steppes, plunge deep into equatorial forests, wage battle at Austerlitz, travel from Rome to the Bicêtre hospital in the footsteps of Rainer Maria Rilke. The Metro map would certainly make a remarkable historical treatise.

Robinson continues. That elderly black man is both accountant and surveyor. He is measuring the unspecified quantity of sweat, blood and death that has determined the design of the Book of Stations.

"Do you understand?"

"No."

"And yet it's very simple. What delights you so much is the result of slavery, of the enslavement of other peoples. Their riches have been transferred and transmuted into steel. They have the most learned alchemists. Now they're making us foot the bill for having been slaves. That's why the old man is pacing up and down the platform."

The next train arrives. It stops. The passengers stream towards the metal doors. Robinson and I get into the same compartment. The train moves off shakily like an old horse.

The slow, certain transformation of landscapes. Blue mingles with grey, the ridges of roofs begin dancing, dancing around the Great Book of Stations.

———

T HE MUSÉE D'ORSAY. People pass through as though they're in a station, literally. They attach very little importance to what they're seeing. And what exactly do they see?

Paintings. Paintings. Paintings.

Processions of paintings, processions of people in front of paintings.

The hyperrealists parade past: people harnessed to the same yoke, like oxen.

Don't hang around, you've got to see as much as you can. Then, quick as a flash, upstairs to the Impressionists! An ascent from purgatory to paradise.

Yet more paintings. Van Gogh ripped off his ear, but you've got to be quick. No one has seen the darkest, most savage painting: *The Potato Eaters*. Not enough time.

Further down, few people have seen *L'Origine du Monde*. The odd visitor has stood in front of it for a minute, chuckling a little, but has then moved off again, double quick.

Si. Two Spanish women. Indeterminate women of indeterminate middle age, midway between two Metro stops. They exclaim touristically. How dreadful!

Women don't like visualizing their sex organs. They avoid talking about them or looking at them. They aren't aware of them. But there's no ignoring them here—they're right in their face.

I look at the women looking at the picture.

How appalling!

They're ashamed. They don't get the chance to see what's always hidden from them. Few people know how to contemplate the intimate. In fact, nobody can. Our perception of origins is located between the stomach and the heart and fluctuates constantly between the two. It gives me a feeling of deep pleasure, a soothing, sexual pleasure. My eyes drift from the dark line to the rounded stomach. I begin to be stirred by what was so frequently celebrated by Baudelaire, fleeces and furs, tresses and tombs, and I'm enraptured by the crotch of the unknown woman, who is revealing to me what she's hiding from others—which is no surprise, as they are hurrying by too fast.

It is to the Spanish women's credit that they stopped to look.

In the end, they chuckle and walk away, not without first calling over the rest of the armada to study the disgraceful painting in close, cackling formation.

You see, I'm much older than I look. I glance at the great master's studio one last time, remove my hat and head off to take paradise by storm.

Paradise: a place where the inscrutable gods sit in state. Their names are Monet and Manet, and I occasionally get them mixed up. Hardly surprising really, I'm a savage, a man from Barbary, a Carthaginian who sacrifices children to Moloch. I wouldn't know which of them painted Rouen cathedral at different times of the day and which painted the luncheon on the grass—and I gaze at the beautiful Hélène, naked and shocking, sitting between her fully clothed men.

She seems to have been posed there by the painter without any concern for propriety or form. Is it the form or the impropriety which is shocking, I wonder again. People walk past, blissfully unaware of the lady surrounded by her handsome gentlemen in their fine suits. What is the point of the blind if they don't sing of the wrath of Achilles or of the man of a thousand turns or of the Sailor of Baghdad. What is the point of the stranger whispering into his mobile. He looks like an angel. Absorption is also a virtue. He is captivated by his call. It links here with there. He is an angel. He is sexless. He doesn't notice Hélène.

The gods are also called Van Gogh.

All I remembered was the severed ear, even if, in Arles, the light still pours down on the little cemetery of Auvers-sur-Oise behind the church, and on the graves of the two brothers, side by side in the light, the rain, the wind blowing over the fields, blowing over the green wheat. Step over the low wall in spring to kiss the lovers united in death, Vincent and Theo under the same magnificent, tormented sky, as poignant as the lovers of Montagne Sainte-Geneviève, sweet Héloïse and her Abélard, who was castrated, then became a monk, according to Villon. Yes, that little cemetery and those two graves brought me a boundless joy that reconciled me to death, men and art. Seeing them reunited like this for an eternity of oblivion kept hope alive and made it possible for me to fall asleep in the gold of morning.

Another night stroll, this time with Zoé. We walked along the banks of the Seine towards Notre Dame. We looked at the carvings and were captivated and enchanted by the infernal bestiary. It even made us tremble with desire and we wondered whether the mythical creatures were protecting this holy site or whether, on the contrary, they were about to swoop down on Paris. We shelved the debate to go for an ice cream at Berthillon's on the Île Saint-Louis.

Zoé was about twenty. I'd met her standing in front of *L'Origine du Monde*: we made fun of the uptight Spanish women and the stuck-up passers-by who barely glanced at the bush of the head-less woman. Zoé couldn't believe that my name was Sinbad and that I had no connection with the famous hero of the same name from Galland's tales. I kept quiet about my secret kinship, my birth across the sea like that of the man from Baghdad. I didn't want to scare her off.

Her eyes beneath her glasses were blue and she had delicate features and full lips. She took great care when expressing herself, as if her thoughts had to take shape first before they were captured by language. I liked that about her: the slightly mannered way she had of speaking, and her Provençal accent, which was as mild and soft as a Roman spring.

We often met in a hotel room on Rue de l'Estrapade, behind the Pantheon. She had the soft skin of a child and barely developed breasts. Her nipples grew larger beneath my tongue and turned purplish when she was fully aroused. I caressed her stomach and kissed it, then buried my face between her thighs, where I lingered, intoxicated by the softness of her vulva and the faint scent emanating from it. I could have lost myself between her legs for hours, but Zoé pulled away and took my cock in her mouth, melting it like an aniseed-flavoured lollipop.

One day, she stole what little money I had and disappeared, leaving me alone in that seedy hotel room. I was intending to leave her, so she went off with my wallet as a form of revenge. But do you take everything an artist, sailor or orphan possesses? Did she really need the paltry sum I owned?

I left the hotel in the early hours of the morning. She hadn't paid the bill and I had no wish to end up at the police station.

That was the way Héloïse and Abélard had parted. The latter was the son of a Breton noble, who'd given up his rights of primogeniture to teach philosophy. As the Notre Dame cloister was dwindling, Abélard broke with his masters and founded a school on Montagne Sainte-Geneviève. His students followed him. He was young, handsome and unusually eloquent. In the evenings, he'd hurry down the mountain to the Seine and return to the house of Canon Fulbert, where he was lodging. The Canon had a very beautiful niece, Héloïse. She became Abélard's diligent student. Naturally, she fell pregnant between one theology lesson and the next. Abélard married her, but the Canon felt that he had been deceived. He hired some ruffians who entered Abélard's room one night and castrated him.

So I went on my way, without Héloïse, still intact. I came down the mountain along Rue Saint-Jacques, walked behind the Sorbonne, then went up Rue Dante, and then Rue du Fouarre: Straw Street. Strange, isn't it, how the streets of Paris always have a hidden meaning, a history. This street used to be covered with straw so that the medieval *escoliers* had somewhere dry to sit when listening to lectures. The street would be packed with students. If a carter took it into his head to drive through during the lectures given by the monks, he would be given a thrashing by the students, who then tipped his load into the road. The city authorities closed off the road with chains to avoid brawls. Classes began in the morning, after mass. Since, during the night, tramps would come and sleep on the straw, they had to be beaten awake before the *fouarre* could be changed for the medieval students.

"How do you know all that?" asked Robinson, my dear, nocturnal companion.

Yes, Robinson had suddenly appeared at the street corner, just like that, just like an apparition. He'd given me some money after I'd told him all about my romantic troubles with the despicable Zoé.

143

"What about Rue Dante? Why is it called that?" asked tall Robinson, whom I hadn't seen for ages and whom I'd missed.

"They say that Dante Alighieri lived here after his flight from Florence."

"Poor Dante, but Paris wasn't the same city back then. People still lived here then, I think."

"In 1309, Dante left Italy. He came here to hear the lessons of Sigier de Brabant. Sitting on the straw in the Rue du Fouarre, he soaked up 'syllogized invidious truths'."

Robinson had hunger pangs; the delicious, heady aroma of kebabs was titillating his nostrils, and that was the only truth he was managing to syllogize.

"I'm starving."

"You should aim for an empty stomach and a light mind. Is there any news of Carlo Moro?"

"Draw a line under that episode, my dear Sinbad. Look around you…"

He gestured at the female students walking back up towards the Sorbonne or the Louis-le-Grand *lycée*.

"No shortage of research subjects."

"No love in the son of the Mohammedan's heart."

"Sounds like Mao, but not really. Like some of the local philosophers. You know who they are. You're the intellectual, after all. Since you've been studying… I mean the guys who once marched from Nation to the Bastille and who now merrily sink cocktails at the Flore and give the Prince advice on procedure."

Of course, I could see that philosophy always ended up in the gutter and turned tricks for media pimps. The companions of Chu En-Lai, Che and Castro had embarked on an anti-Muslim crusade. Anybody whose ancestor had set foot in a mosque was a potential fascist, a neo-Nazi killer of good women, a destroyer of freedoms, an emasculator and a genocidist. It wasn't easy for me or Robinson to be called potential despots: we'd fled the tyranny of Ubu, the Grand Inquisitor and the Top Mullah. It was depressing to be lumped together with veil agitators, Qur'an devourers and Osama's Septembrists and chucked into the Seine. But that's the West for you: it has a boundless capacity for generalization.

XIII

Hérode didn't like anyone. There was one exception: an Angora cat called Proust, which he'd just taken in and which went everywhere with him; he carried it clasped to his breast, stroking it and declaiming a poem written during the night. The poem always appealed to the cat, which was his best, most discerning and loudest purring critic.

"Oh! If only everyone could be like Proust!"

"But, darling, Proust is a cat."

"France, you're really getting on my nerves!"

He would then lock himself in France's small apartment on the ground floor of the apartment block, and wouldn't come out again that day. He put in some more time on *Le Bouton d'Anaïs*, then polished it further. The workaholic spent hours shining up that novel which had been rejected by every publishing house worthy of the title, and then, abandoning this by now almost lifeless work, he got down to his collection of poetry, *Il y a du Bouleau*, immortal pieces celebrating the Russian forests. Hérode, born in Mali, dreamt of the deathless Russia of authors such as Tolstoy, Solzhenitsyn and Pasternak.

"My dear Sinbad, open your eyes, open them wide!"

Hérode then began obsessively consulting Proust, who didn't much like his heavy-handed petting and hightailed it to the living room where he hid under an armchair.

"Come back, Proust; here, dear Proust, come here!"

But Proust didn't come back and Hérode, who felt that his authority was being flouted, seethed with anger.

"True literature doesn't give a damn about minor works penned by your hacks! You should read Tolstoy, Yesenin or Mayakovsky instead, geniuses we should be imitating the way Leonardo imitated Verrocchio. I'll bet you've never been to Florence, my dear Sinbad."

"I know the city of the Pazzi very well."

"Who are the Pazzi?"

Hérode had never set foot in Florence. Since he didn't have a residence permit, there was no way he could leave French territory. The only journey the great poet was likely to make was to be bundled onto a charter flight under the indifferent gaze of the other passengers.

One day, France took me to one side and said, "Hérode is beside himself with jealousy. He thinks you... Sinbad, you'll have to leave. I know someone who'll rent you a studio in Montmartre. Sometimes he flies into such terrible rages. He thinks everyone is against him, and that no one recognizes his genius. He's under so much pressure, you understand. If he didn't have Proust, he'd have thrown himself out of the window by now."

"You live on the ground floor!"

"You do understand, don't you, Sinbad? An African in Paris. With a white woman. If you saw the way people look at us in the street. Don't forget what happened on the seventeenth of October, 1961. Four hundred odd Algerians in the Seine and Papon the Nazi congratulated by De Gaulle. And long before that, the Vichy collaborators were in Paris too, don't forget. This city doesn't like strangers, Sinbad."

The City of Lights was a myth that had been exported all over the world in the early twentieth century. What's more, it was the only French creation, along with Camembert and Bordeaux, that was in high demand from the American tourists praising the light in August. Sartre, Camus, Foucault and Derrida were forgotten, Mondrian and Zadkine tossed aside. All that was left were the Sollers, the rearguard Combazes and the not-so-new Nouvels. A depressing period and a depressing city which now tracked down foreigners, drove out all the Picassos and Modiglianis, and shoved them onto planes so that they could be spewed out somewhere else. Of course, there was still the American *Way of Life* with its Hollywood bubblegum, a lure which worked for some overseas writers from the Caribbean who championed *Créolité* and other types of nonsense rubbished by Hérode as he stroked Proust.

So I took up residence in the heart of the myth, in Montmartre, in a strange, lopsided house on Rue d'Orchampt. I liked the district and the low rent. When the weather was good, I walked up Rue Lepic, past the Moulin de la Galette, took Rue Norvins or Rue Sainte-Rustique to Rue du Mont-Cenis, which used to be called Rue Saint-Denis. I always sat at a table in the same café, opposite the tourist shops whose windows displayed ridiculous T-shirts printed with an Eiffel Tower or a Sacré-Coeur. The street looked like a souk, which rather appealed to me, and I swore that one day I'd visit the caravanserais of Aleppo and the huge market in Damascus.

In Rue du Mont-Cenis, I watched hordes of young women from every country in the world strutting past in God's light. Another man might have complained about this never-ending influx of people, the continual upheaval endangering the district, disfiguring it so badly that it made you wonder whether the Commune had ever really happened here, if the blood that once flowed here hadn't really been grenadine, if Montmartre was still hidden beneath Montmartre. This thorny enigma was likely to cause a new rift among the *bobos*, the bohemian bourgeois who had made their money from the film industry and were now pushing their prams along the streets of the 'Butte Rouge'.

Me, I didn't care, I was as blasé as a Roman. I'd gained composure. I no longer believed in anything; I didn't even miss Vitalia any more. I was lost to love, I devoured women the way other men might eat a pastry. Do you ask a chocolate-covered cream puff for emotion? I just watched the prettiest tourists and pounced on the one who seemed the most accommodating. They were all looking for a carnal change of scene, the lyricism peddled by Doisneau with his postcards, the lethal myth that Paris is the perfect place to fall in love. A little like Venice and its Bridge of Sighs, where the fools would kiss, blissfully unaware that the passage was once used to take prisoners to the cells known as "the Leads", hence the sighs. The same is true of Paris. A field of ruins where women and children were massacred in 1871; the Seine, a common grave into which they tossed Algerians in 1961; the Hôtel Lutétia, first headquarters of the Gestapo and then a destination for concentration-camp survivors. Paris, the city of lovers.

Anyway, I liked to spend my nights in Montmartre, walking along Rue Poulbot, following the decrepit ramparts of Montmartre to a wintry Place du Tertre in the rain, far from the city's din, lonely as the Devil in my long black coat. I became one with the walls, the cobblestones, the air. I was a damned soul. One evening, when there was a crescent moon, a woman in a hoodie who looked like Vitalia walked towards me. The look she gave me made me lower my eyes in shame. As dark as the lady in Shakespeare's sonnets, she was waiting alone in front of Saint-Pierre de Montmartre, cowled like a nun. She lowered her hood and entered the church, which is dwarfed by the hideous Sacré-Coeur. Any right-thinking Montmartrian would have reduced it to rubble if they could.

I followed her, my heart beating erratically. I was convinced I was going to die. I walked into the stone conch, which was filled with an atmosphere of great peace. She was walking in front of me like Beatrice. I longed with all my soul to be a poet too, so that I could recognize real love, my one true love. Vitalia made the sign

150

THE NEW ADVENTURES OF SINBAD THE SAILOR

of the cross before the altar, and stopped in front of the stele to Adele of Savoy: this Queen of France had founded the abbey and used to come here to pray for a kingdom which wasn't yet hitting the headlines, but probably had a clearer idea of its own identity.

It was Vitalia, just taller and even darker. She was now holding a candle which she lit. The candlelight spread beneath the vaults, then faded. Only her face burned like the Tree, the holy Olive Tree of the East and the West. Then the flame went out and I lost her in the dark.

XIV

I N THE RUE DU MONT-CENIS, I was approached by a very dark-skinned girl, who wanted to draw my portrait. A student at the École des Beaux-Arts, she was sketching tourists to bring in a little extra cash. I struck a pose and the beautiful young woman drew my picture, enraptured by my sailor's profile. After I'd paid her, she sat down at my table and ordered a mint cordial. Her name was Thamara, and she had black eyes, wavy hair, and a slender build. When I related my sordid exploits, she laughed a lot. I didn't leave out a single thing that had happened to me since I'd come into the world. In her mind's eye, I acquired a fantastical dimension and became a kind of mythical creature, a fictional fantasy character, a harlequin from the *commedia dell'arte*.

Thamara laughed again when I told her about my enslavement on the beaches of Cetraro, my stay at the Villa Medici with its gallery of eccentrics, those gingerbread artists who filled the avenues of the now spiritless stately home, where what wit remained was that malicious, facetious brand of humour which at times gave rise to mockery. Thamara's expression darkened. She believed that this was the kind of petty ridicule that sometimes paved the way for the Master of Curses whom the Gnostics called the Demiurge and who had created the Cave where men were born, quarrelled with each other, then tortured each other to death. In the Cave slept the Seven of Ephesus, the righters of wrongs whose awakening would herald the end of time.

Thamara knew the Bible and the Gnostic writings by heart. She interpreted the history of the world and the great natural disasters in terms of the power of the Demiurge or of his opposite, the childlike spirit that sometimes took human form in people like me, who lived superficial lives with no ties, artists whose inability to be serious provided some protection against the world's madness. At other times, it was the Demiurge who took possession of men, filling them with anger; they would then set about each other and become like rabid dogs.

I didn't understand everything Thamara told me. She was a woman of her times, in love with manufactured ideas, strange beliefs combining energy and flow, a superstitious mishmash, but I knew that the young woman thought that I, Sinbad, was a figure of the utmost importance, a trump card, a positive value in an absurd world. I didn't believe it, of course, but I loved Thamara, another wonder encountered along my road of exile, whether it led to Damascus, Bosra, Constantinople or Jerusalem.

I addressed my Letter to the Ephesians to Thamara's body, since that princess from one of the books of the Bible was as beautiful as Solomon's mistress, the queen of Sheba, whose legs were slender black columns and whose eyes were veiled doves. Her hair was a flock of goats on the mountainside and her teeth were shining fragments of ivory. Thamara, my sister, my spouse, delighted my heart. Milk and honey flowed in abundance under her tongue, as though in some paradise beyond my wildest dreams. She was like an enclosed garden, my sister, my spouse, a garden from Lebanon where all manner of fragrances rose into the air. And I entered this cloister and plucked the fruit of the pomegranate tree. Through the middle flowed a sealed fountain whose waters formed paths where I lost myself between palm trees, privet hedge, myrrh and incense, and the blood-red flowerbeds where saffron, nard and

Cinnamomum grew and where I meditated in silence, a lover of virgins and perfumes.

Thamara was as slim-waisted as a palm tree and her breasts were bunches of grapes that I pressed between my lips. Madly in love, we went travelling.

We visited Damascus, in Syria, where the area around Bab Touma, the Gate of St Thomas, takes on a festive mood at night, and the girls and boys walk, arms entwined, their hair blowing in the wind, as they do in Paris. I was fascinated by the dusky, slender women, their dark eyes outlined in kohl, who brushed by us in the narrow streets of the Medina.

We slept in a house which had a murmuring fountain in a patio straight out of the *Arabian Nights*. The house, with its Damascene two-tone masonry, had been run first by an English woman, who eventually sold it to a young Christian man. In the evening, we would go up onto the terrace and gaze at the Minaret of the Bride on the far horizon under the stars: I was the Hebrews and she was Pharaoh. Then we embraced, before falling asleep to the singing of the muezzins, whose melodies mingled in the night, like a strange alcohol, with the perfume of a bougainvillea.

The following day, we visited the Great Mosque of Damascus, whose minaret we had seen from afar. The outer wall was surrounded by stalls selling recently made marquetry and Qur'ans printed in Iran. Droves of women shrouded in black veils and crying out in Persian flocked into the mosque and gathered in the chamber where the head of Imam Hussein lay behind a silver grille, wrapped in strange fabrics. I too walked over to the tomb in fascination and gazed at the precious head of the Prophet's grandson, wondering if it was genuine, then walked away overcome by a premonition of misfortune, an irrational fear of death brought on by that vile relic.

As for Thamara, she wept at the thought of the face battered by Caliph Yazid I who, as the story goes, hit the corpse's lips, declaring: "We would have been content with the submission of the inhabitants of Iraq without this murder. But you, Hussein, broke the bonds of kinship and became a rebel!"

A witness is said to have replied: "Get that stick away from the mouth that was kissed so often by the Prophet, his grandfather!"

Yazid was allegedly irritated by these words, but spared Ali, Hussein's son, and his family.

I wondered if Hussein's head had been preserved out of devotion for the holy man or to serve as an example to the rebels. Wasn't the mosque actually built half a century after his death to expiate that founding murder? I was impressed by the constant stream of Iranian pilgrims who had come to kiss the mausoleum of the martyr of Karbala, weeping bitter tears as if they were mourning the death of a father or much-loved brother. These emotional outbursts left me cold. I couldn't relate to such overblown displays of grief, which I had a feeling were put on. What was described as religious fervour was, in fact, an awful drama in which the actor was manipulated into playing his part so well that he was unable to get out of character after the performance. Did those men and women return to normal life after they left the mosque? Did they stop to look in a mirror and dry their tears, tidy their hair or reapply their makeup? When you see a man praying, how much of it is an act? Can we believe in faith if it calls attention to itself?

Thamara had taken my hand. She was dressed from head to toe in a grey abaya without which she wouldn't have been able to enter the mosque, the domain of ancient widows, mourning women and the Fates. And the actors, oh, the actors! Dance for us, you puppets, clowns and harlequins, dance! A sincere prayer needs no pretence, no bogus grief or public rapture. Pleasure is best taken in silence, by my faith as a sailor and a lover.

We came out into the white-marble courtyard which reflected the sun, the cloudless sky and the green and gold mosaics depicting a paradise of palms and fruit, a promise of a magnificent afterlife, surrounded by a village or ancient city. The trees bore pearls, or they might have been fruit, grapes used to make wine for the best of men. These grapes have been mistaken for beautiful virgins: the Islamic afterlife holds out no promise of women, to my great despair, just a goblet of aged wine and divine intoxication on the banks of the Barada River, flowing through Sham from the Anti-Lebanon mountains. The martyrs themselves, who have been changed into trees, are the ones bearing the heady nectar in the tranquil eternity of their plant-like existence.

And so I lost myself in the Garden of Earthly Delights, accompanied by my sister-spouse, my army, Thamara, whose name is also a fruit that brings oblivion.

Then we walked across the courtyard and ended up beneath the Bayt al-Mal, an octagon covered in mosaics the same colour as those of the mosque, standing on Corinthian columns like a tall wader over a pool of milk. It was once used as the treasury of the Faithful, storing donations used for worship, maintaining the mosque and preparing for the wars that plunged Damascus into turmoil for centuries and resulted in its ruin on many an occasion.

The mosque was burnt down in the eleventh century, destroyed in the fifteenth by Tamerlane and then burnt down again under the Ottoman Empire at the end of the nineteenth century. All the floor mosaics were ruined and replaced by white marble in imitation of the marble facing on the walls of the Umayyad Mosque in Aleppo, which we visited next and which we thought looked like an exact replica of the one in Damascus, although there were infinitesimal variations between the two, creating a divide. The former was Roman and Byzantine at heart, while the latter, due to a strange and obsessive perfectionism, had become Arab and as ochre as the sands of Palmyra. So there you could hope for a paradise filled with virgins instead of ancient bunches of grapes. Vines don't grow in the desert, so the believer giving up his life for an idea needs some other kind of compensation. God is an abstract concept, become flesh, guiding the praying man through the icy solitude of the dunes. Mohammed's religion is demanding, sober, cold. It doesn't permit identification with its deity and it offers no comfort. It is conveyed by words, the text is chanted until it takes shape in the believer's mind, like a vast stele on the path of desolation. That is the miracle of the Qur'an: starry words against the dark, empty dome of the sky.

WE LEFT DAMASCUS for Aleppo.
The town was like a vast field of stones, rising from the rock and stretching towards the fortress built by Sayf al-Dawla. Standing on the ramparts of the Citadel, we amused ourselves by pointing out the souk, and the various khans we'd visited the night before which, in some cases, remained empty after being abandoned by the merchants and customers of past centuries. It was as if, after five thousand years of existence, the town were slowly turning into a fossil, keeping only its mineral shell, like those strange prehistoric molluscs of which all that remains is a solid imprint, the snapshot of a creature which died at the dawn of time.

Other gaudier caravanserais could be discovered by the few tourists who strayed into the covered lanes of the old souk while walking beside the Umayyad Mosque, which was superficially similar to the one in Damascus but more human, intimate and alive. Built by the same caliph, it was also destroyed on numerous occasions, but history appeared to have no dominion over it. It too remained enclosed inside a gangue which had saved it from damage. It was just one more fossil visited by archaeologists of the faith who prostrated themselves before it five times a day, having performed their ablutions around a fountain that was the spitting image of the one in the mosque of Damascus but ochre in hue, the prevailing colour of the town, inspired by the immensity of the Mesopotamian desert.

The town afforded some magnificent sights. I walked around as if in a dream, pretending to be Al-Mutanabbi, that arrogant courtier and poet, or Al-Farabi, the physician and illustrious citizen of the ancient city of Halab, the daughter of Abraham the shepherd. He preferred to milk his goats in solitude and their milk still flows over the marble of the great mosque, between the ochre and grey contours of the labyrinth, transformed into a place of hypnotic glory by the muezzin's song, which was lovelier than the one in Damascus. This singing carried me towards unattainable spheres, so overwhelming my soul that I came down with a high fever and was confined to bed for several days in a nice hotel in the Christian district of Jdeideh. They even sent for a doctor who diagnosed a slight cough, probably brought on by exposing my simple, feminine soul to the complexity of a thousand-year-old city. When I'd recovered, I went back to exploring the narrow streets of the town.

Thamara went everywhere with me in that city of soap bars. She stayed by my side and followed me to give me reassurance, as if holding a child's hand on the way to school. She kissed me in Aleppo's bazaar, under the mocking gaze of the merchants, who invited us into their shops, a ritual we willingly accepted before coming back out, slightly disenchanted, our bags crammed full of multi-coloured fabrics, the finest in the world, of course, and bars and bars of Aleppo soap, which surely needs no advertisement, enough of the stuff, in fact, to clean a whole regiment of brutish soldiers. As well as priceless trinkets that were not without value (indeed, noble Sinbad, as a man of taste, a fellow Arab, and a worthy descendant of Emir Abdelkader, you must appreciate the exquisite craftsmanship, the fine work of the artisan who sacrificed his sight and reason to it, a man whose wife ran off with his brother and who died of despair after creating this piece!) which, without a shadow of a doubt, would complement the dark, bewitching eyes of the houri accompanying a great lord like Sinbad, who would bring dishonour on himself if he left without giving one of these necklaces to his wife, or a silver bracelet to adorn the slim, aristocratic wrist of that gazelle, a silk scarf to cover that regal throat, a veil woven in Homs (before it was bombed!) by young girls with eyes as keen as birds of prey, who were dismissed from the job when they were of marriageable age, in other words, when they were twelve, or perhaps thirteen at the most, since, if you left it any longer, they would wither like flowers after dewfall and end up like elderly Fates, their claw-like fingers snagging on the warp as they spat out their chewing tobacco on the floor.

———

BEFORE LEAVING ALEPPO, we had one last drink at the Baron. Agatha Christie and Lawrence of Arabia had once stayed at this hotel, founded in 1911. The latter had displayed a truly British sense of style by leaving without paying his bill. This was now a framed relic in one of the lounges, like Poe's purloined letter, the only difference being that the thief himself had put his name to his crime and had then revelled in a life of compulsive lying by writing *The Seven Pillars of Wisdom*, a farcical story about the Arab revolt led by a certain Faisal. I came down hard on Lawrence, who'd felt real affection for the Middle East and the Arab men he'd desired. He'd wanted to serve two masters, his desire and the British Empire; the Empire had won in the end and he'd ended up alone, swindled of his dreams, in England, where all he could do was build up his legend to avoid dying in vain.

The barman was eager to please, since no one stayed there any more and the hotel was on the verge of collapse—the Baron seemed to have been deserted since the Second World War. He headed over to an enormous machine which looked like an old fridge and began trying to get it to work. The ancient piece of machinery was supposed to produce cool air. A loud throbbing sound filled the room and a little hot air brushed past our faces. When I remarked that the machine was producing more noise than comfort, the barman ducked down behind his counter and triumphantly re-emerged with a bucket of ice cubes. He disappeared behind the box of tricks, opened it and poured in the contents of the receptacle. We waited a few minutes for the magic to work, but nothing happened. We didn't want to upset our host, so we exclaimed that the air flowing into the room was the coolest, nicest air we had ever felt. Looking more cheerful, the barman beamed: the Baron had lost none of its former glory.

A very tall man came into the bar and headed over to us.

"I'm your driver, Mr Sinbad. I was told you wanted to visit Palmyra. It's very beautiful. Very beautiful. Good choice. And then Bosra, if I've got it right. Oh! the theatre in Bosra is such a wonderful…"

"Robinson!"

"Aha, I had you there, didn't I?"

"What are you doing in Syria?"

"I prefer Ubu's kingdom to Kaposi's republic. That French walking-disaster… that caricature of a president."

"I agree: that windbag is extremely tiresome."

"I got my bundle and my hooded coat and decided to escape to Egypt. We're the Jews of this century, Sinbad. From Egypt, I crossed borders and countries and here I am in Sham, where I'm working as a tour guide for lovers like you."

He took Thamara's hand and kissed it in pure Louis XIV style. Dear Robinson was well bred and well educated. He was certified and vaccinated, no one could be more French. That Ostrogoth, cutpurse, punter of Phynance and crooked arms-dealer had got himself elected president of France by setting fire to the suburbs and by anathematizing foreigners and the poor. He was preparing to redefine the identity of that now obsolete country that was discovering its Texan and Bushist destiny, while America was electing a black man as president.

"You should have tried America, Robinson. It's an up-and-coming country, not like Kaposi's republic."

"That villain is getting ready to collect our DNA to purify his racial pyramid. Whites at the top, then dogs and cats at the bottom. Negroes and dirty North-African Arabs like you and me are destined for the catacombs and solitary confinement. You know, I admire his discourse."

"Aha! The long-winded spiel about Africa and the Immobile Man. The return of the same, the eternal return. A little badly digested Nietzsche, a great deal of stupidity, the same stale old ideas and France is preparing to reach for glory in the twenty-first century. Hallelujah!"

"I preferred Syria, it's a more moderate country, after all."

"You're not kidding, Robinson."

———

S LUMPED in battered armchairs, we drank Cokes with Robinson, who then drove us into the desert. Thamara's parents gave her a nice little sum of money every year to help her complete her world tour, so she was a wealthy student. Being poor as Job, I went with her to defend her in case of attack by the Syrian forces, who were much feared in the area but lacked any real strength.

The black Jeeps that drove up and down the country's roads and the many barely concealed military zones strengthened the myth of a country governed by an iron fist in an oriental glove. The aim was to ensure that the population believed this, because it kept them under the yoke more effectively and allowed them to revel in their imaginary strength. You could tyrannize your own people, but you couldn't strip them of their dignity. These pretences created by Arab countries, their senseless rivalries and imagined wars, served to maintain the illusion of past grandeur. Lawrence had realized that when he incited a few tribes to conquer the Ottoman Empire for the greater good of the British and the French. All those countries were colonial pawns, as feeble and agitated as defenceless old men.

I didn't give a damn about international politics. I was an anarchist of love, a student rebel from 1968 stranded in the middle of the twenty-first century, an unrepentant peace-lover. Another small detail: Thamara was Jewish and should never have set foot in Syria. However, an employee at the consulate gave her a visa because he thought, with a somewhat twisted logic, that if his nation's authorities were prepared to torture prisoners for the Americans, who were their sworn enemies, he didn't see why an honest girl, whether Jewish by faith or not, shouldn't set foot in Syria which, in his view, was the best country in the world, and deserved to be seen by our cousins.

The employee even instructed Thamara to visit the museum in Damascus, which had a third-century synagogue on display as evidence of the region's rich heritage. And so the synagogue was visited by two Semites who could admire its frescos showing scenes from the Talmud. Endless depictions of patriarchs and their children extended across the walls adorned with dazzling paintings at variance with all the aesthetic canons in force in late antiquity: this was a kind of manifesto, a protest against the official art whose centre of power was moving further East, with its childish myths and a religion that mimicked theirs in tow. In one of the walls, the niche for the Holy Ark showed the direction of Jerusalem, the sacrifice of Abraham and the hand of God.

XV

THE PEOPLE OF CARTHAGO, happy to swallow yet another piece of nonsense, had been told that the war had ended in the early 1960s. In fact, it would never be over—even worse, it was reaching its tertiary phase and was in danger of paralysing the sufferers, leaving them aphasic and teetering on the brink of nothingness. The inhabitants of Carthago were like zombies anyway: their soul and consciousness had been amputated, they'd been tyrannized and terrorized like laboratory rats, and they'd been injected with highly noxious poisons on numerous occasions, and almost exterminated. The survivors had proliferated again, as if driven by a lust for life, refusing to give in, but immediately a new natural disaster or a new war annihilated the generation that had risen from the flames like sparks blown against the milky darkness of space, like stars about to shine brightly, a promise of happiness or rebirth. The sky immediately grew dark as a result of fresh fires that had taken hold, stoked by pyromaniac firemen, which might have amused a twisted mind, a God like the one who had created the Sleeper and his dog. But was it even the same deity?

Maybe Thamara was right: a Demiurge was mocking humanity, causing mankind to perish in the flames of a bogus paradise, while the distant, infinite-creator God was helplessly watching this tangled mass of violence, murder and genocidal rage, twiddling his thumbs like an old man in his dotage.

Now the old man had finally woken up and had decided to erase his lousy first draft.

This was all very unsettling, and I opened my heart to Thamara, who tried her best to reassure me, modelling herself on Khadija, the Prophet's first wife.

But I was trembling with cold more than amazement and my beautiful Thamara covered me with her body, while the sun burned the stones as if a flameless fire still projected the bright, hot colours of the inferno: in the same way, the history of mankind projected images of its own past and recreated a present out of legends by gathering ancient glimmers of light, like dead stars shining on in the sky long after their death.

I wasn't easily influenced, yet I allowed myself to sink into a fearful lethargy that took hold of my mind and darkened my memory. The fever reclaimed me. During the night, Sinbad, my ancient double, came to me and the storyteller began his tale:

"When I had returned to Baghdad, I indulged in sport, pleasure and delight, rejoicing greatly in my gains, profits and benefits, and forgot all I had experienced and suffered until I began to think again of travelling to see foreign countries and islands. Having made my resolve, I bought valuable merchandise suited to a sea voyage, packed up my bales, and journeyed from Baghdad to Basra. I walked along the shore and saw a large, tall, and goodly ship, newly fitted. It pleased me and I bought it. Then I hired a captain and crew, over whom I set some of my slaves and pages as superintendents, and loaded my bales on the ship. Then a group of merchants joined me, loaded their bales on the ship, and paid me the freight. We set out in all joy and cheerfulness, rejoicing in the prospect of a safe and prosperous voyage, and sailed from sea to sea and from island to island, landing to see the sights of the islands and towns and to sell and buy.

"We continued in this fashion until one day we came to a large uninhabited island, waste and desolate, except for a vast white dome. The merchants landed to look at the dome, which was in reality a huge Rukh's egg, but, not knowing what it was, they struck it with stones, and when they broke it, much fluid ran out of it, and the young Rukh appeared inside. They drew it out of the shell, slaughtered it, and took from it a great deal of meat. While this was going on, I was on the ship, uninformed and unaware of it until one of the passengers came to me and said, 'Sir, go and look at that egg, which we thought to be a dome.' I went to look at the egg and arrived just as the merchants were striking it. I cried out to them, 'Don't do this, for the Rukh will come, demolish our ship, and destroy us all.' But they did not heed my words.

"While they were thus engaged, the sun suddenly disappeared, and the day grew dark, as if a dark cloud was passing above us. We raised our heads to see what had veiled the sun and saw that it was the Rukh's wings that had blocked the sunlight and made the day dark, for when the Rukh came and saw its egg broken, it cried out at us, and its mate came, and they circled above the ship, shrieking with voices louder than thunder. I called out to the captain and the sailors, saying, 'Push off the ship, and let us escape before we perish.' The captain hurried and, as soon as the merchants had embarked, unfastened the ship and sailed away from the island. When the Rukhs saw that we were on the open sea, they disappeared for a while.

"We sailed, making speed, in the desire to leave their land behind and escape from them, but suddenly they caught up with us, each carrying in its talons a huge rock from a mountain. Then the male bird threw its rock on us, but the captain steered the ship aside, and the rock missed it by a little distance, and fell into the water with such force that we saw the bottom of the sea, and the ship went up and down, almost out of control. Then the female bird threw on us its rock, which was smaller than the first, but as it had been ordained, it fell on the stern of the ship, smashed it, sent the rudder flying in twenty pieces, and threw all the passengers into the sea.

"I struggled for dear life to save myself until the Almighty God provided me with one of the wooden planks of the ship, to which I clung and, getting on it, began to paddle with my feet, while the wind and the waves helped me forward. The ship had sunk near an island in the middle of the sea, and fates cast me, according to God's will, on that island, where I landed, like a dead man, on my last breath from extreme hardship and fatigue and hunger and thirst. I threw myself on the seashore and lay for a while until I began to recover myself and feel better. Then I walked in the island and found that it was like one of the gardens of Paradise. Its trees were laden with fruits, its streams flowing, and its birds singing the glory of the Omnipotent, Everlasting One. There was an abundance of trees, fruits and all kinds of flowers. So I ate of the fruits until I satisfied my hunger and drank of the streams until I quenched my thirst, and I thanked the Almighty God and praised Him.

"I sat in the island until it was evening, and night approached, without seeing anyone or hearing any voice. I was still feeling almost dead from fatigue and fear; so I lay down and slept till the morning. Then I got up and walked among the trees until I came to a spring of running water, beside which sat a comely old man clad with a waistcloth made of tree leaves. I said to myself, 'Perhaps the old man has landed on the island, being one of those who have been shipwrecked.' I drew near to him and saluted him, and he returned my salutation with a sign but remained silent. I said to him, 'Old man, why are you sitting here?' He moved his head mournfully and motioned with his hand, meaning to say, 'Carry me on your shoulders, and take me to the other side of the stream.' I said to myself, 'I will do this old man a favour and transport him to the other side of the stream, for God may reward me for it.' I went to him, carried him on my shoulders, and took him to the place to which he had pointed. I said to him, 'Get down at your ease,' but he did not

168

get off my shoulders. Instead, he wrapped his legs around my neck, and when I saw that their hide was as black and rough as that of a buffalo, I was frightened and tried to throw him off. But he pressed his legs around my neck and choked my throat until I blacked out and fell unconscious to the ground, like a dead man. He raised his legs and beat me on the back and shoulders, causing me intense pain. I got up, feeling tired from the burden, and he kept riding on my shoulders and motioning me with his hand to take him among the trees to the best of the fruits, and whenever I disobeyed him, he gave me, with his feet, blows more painful than the blows of the whip. He continued to direct me with his hand to any place he wished to go, and I continued to take him to it until we made our way among the trees to the middle of the island. Whenever I loitered or went leisurely, he beat me, for he held me like a captive. He never got off my shoulders, day or night, urinating and defecating on me, and whenever he wished to sleep, he would wrap his legs around my neck and sleep a little, then arise and beat me, and I would get up quickly, unable to disobey him because of the severity of the pain I suffered from him. I continued with him in this condition, suffering from extreme exhaustion and blaming myself for having taken pity on him and carried him on my shoulders. I said to myself, 'I have done this person a good deed, and it has turned evil to myself. By God, I will never do good to anyone, as long as I live,' and I began to beg, at every turn and every step, the Almighty God for death, because of the severity of my fatigue and distress.

"I continued in this situation for some time until one day I came with him to a place in the island where there was an abundance of gourds, many of which were dry. I selected one that was large and dry, cut it at the neck and cleansed it. Then I went with it to a grapevine and filled it with the juice of the grapes. Then I plugged the gourd, placed it in the sun, and left it there several days until the juice turned into wine, from which I began to

169

drink every day in order to find some relief from the exhausting burden of that obstinate devil, for I felt invigorated whenever I was intoxicated.

"One day he saw me drinking and signed to me with his hand, meaning to say, 'What is this?' I said to him, 'This is an excellent drink that invigorates and delights.' Then I ran with him and danced among the trees, clapping my hands and singing and enjoying myself, in the exhilaration of intoxication. When he saw me in that state, he motioned to me to give him the gourd, in order that he might drink from it. Being afraid of him, I gave it to him, and he drank all that was in it and threw it to the ground. Then he became enraptured and began to shake on my shoulders, and as he became extremely intoxicated and sank into torpor, all his limbs and muscles relaxed, and he began to sway back and forth on my shoulders. When I realized that he was drunk and that he was unconscious, I held his feet and loosened them from my neck, and stooping with him, I sat down and threw him to the ground, hardly believing that I had delivered myself from him. But, fearing that he might recover from his drunkenness and harm me, I took a huge stone from among the trees, came to him, struck him on the head as he lay asleep, mingling his flesh with his blood, and killed him. May God have no mercy on him!

"Then I walked in the island, feeling relieved, until I came back to the spot on the seashore where I had been before. I remained there for some time, eating of the fruits of the island and drinking of its water and waiting for a ship to pass by, until one day, as I sat thinking about what had happened to me and reflecting on my situation, saying to myself, 'I wonder whether God will preserve me and I will return to my country and be reunited with my relatives and friends,' a ship suddenly approached from the middle of the roaring, raging sea and continued until it set anchor at the island, and its passengers landed. I walked toward them, and when they saw me, they all quickly hurried to me and gathered around me, inquiring about my situation and the reason for my coming to that island. I told them about my situation and what had happened to me, and they were amazed and said, 'The man who rode on your shoulders is called the Old Man of the Sea, and no one was ever beneath his limbs and escaped safely, except yourself. God be praised for your safety.' Then they brought me some food, and I ate until I had enough, and they gave me some clothes, which I wore to make myself decent. Then they took me with them in the ship, and we journeyed many days and nights until fate drove us to a city of tall buildings, all of which overlooked the sea. This city is called the City of the Apes, and when night comes, the inhabitants come out of the gates overlooking the sea and, embarking in boats and ships, spend the night there, for fear that the apes may descend on them from the mountains.

"I landed, and while I was enjoying the sights of the city, the ship sailed, without my knowledge. I regretted having disembarked in that city, remembering my companions and what had happened to us with the apes the first and the second time, and I sat down, weeping and mourning. Then one of the inhabitants came to me and said, 'Sir, you seem to be a stranger in this place.' I replied, 'Yes, I am a poor stranger. I was in a ship that anchored here, and I landed to see the sights of the city, and when I went back, I could not find the ship.' He said, 'Come with us and get into the boat, for if you spend the night here, the apes will destroy you.' I said, 'I hear and obey,' and got up immediately and embarked with them in the boat, and they pushed it off from the shore until we were a mile away. We spent the night in the boat, and when it was morning, they returned to the city, landed, and each of them went to his business. Such has been their habit every night, and whoever remains behind in the city at night, the apes come and destroy him. During the day, the apes go outside the city and eat of the fruits in the orchards and sleep in the mountains until the evening, at which time they return to the city.

"The city is located in the farthest parts of the land of the blacks. One of the strangest things I experienced in the inhabitants' treatment of me was as follows. One of those with whom I spent the night in the boat said to me, 'Sir, you are a stranger here. Do you have any craft you can work at?' I replied, 'No, by God, my friend, I have no trade and no handicraft, for I was a merchant, a man of property and wealth, and I owned a ship laden with abundant goods, but it was wrecked in the sea, and everything in it sank. I escaped from drowning only by the grace of God, for He provided me with a plank of wood on which I floated and saved myself.' When he heard my words, he got up and brought me a cotton bag and said, 'Take this bag, fill it with pebbles from the shore, and go with a group of the inhabitants, whom I will help you join and to whom I will commend you, and do as they do, and perhaps you will gain what will help you return to your country.'

"Then he took me with him until we came outside the city, where I picked small pebbles until the bag was filled. Soon a group of men emerged from the city, and he put me in their charge and commended me to them, saying, 'This man is a stranger. Take him with you and teach him how to pick, so that he may gain his living and God may reward you.' They said, 'We hear and obey,' and they welcomed me and took me with them, and proceeded, each carrying a cotton bag like mine, filled with pebbles. We walked until we came to a spacious valley, full of trees so tall that no one could climb them. The valley was also full of apes, which, when they saw us, fled and climbed up into the trees. The men began to pelt the apes with the pebbles from the bags, and the apes began to pluck the fruits of those trees and to throw them at the men, and as I looked at the fruits the apes were throwing, I found that they were coconuts.

"When I saw what the men were doing, I chose a huge tree full of apes and, advancing to it, began to pelt them, while they plucked the nuts and threw them at me. I began to collect the nuts

172

as the men did, and before my bag was empty of pebbles, I had collected plenty of nuts. When the men finished the work, they gathered together all the nuts, and each of them carried as many as he could, and we returned to the city, arriving before the end of the day. Then I went to my friend, who had helped me join the group, and gave him all the nuts I had gathered, thanking him for his kindness, but he said to me, 'Take the nuts, sell them, and use the money.' Then he gave me a key to a room in his house, saying, 'Keep there whatever is left of the nuts, and go out every day with the men, as you did today, and of what you bring with you separate the bad and sell them, and use the money, but keep the best in that room, so that you may gather enough to help you with your voyage.' I said to him, 'May the Almighty God reward you,' and did as he told me, going out daily to gather pebbles, join the men, and do as they did, while they commended me to each other and guided me to the trees bearing the most nuts. I continued in this manner for some time, during which I gathered a great store of excellent coconuts and sold a great many, making a good deal of money, with which I bought whatever I saw and liked. So I thrived and felt happy in that city.

"One day, as I was standing on the seashore, a ship arrived, cast anchor, and landed a group of merchants, who proceeded to sell and buy and exchange goods for coconuts and other commodities. I went to my friend and told him about the ship that had arrived and said that I would like to return to my country. He said, 'It is for you to decide.' So I thanked him for his kindness and bade him farewell. Then I went to the ship, met the captain, and, booking a passage, loaded my store of coconuts on the ship. We set out and continued to sail from sea to sea and from island to island, and at every island we landed, I sold and traded with coconuts until God compensated me with more than I had possessed before and lost.

"Among other places we visited, we came to an island abounding in cinnamon and pepper. Some people told us that they had seen on every cluster of peppers a large leaf that shades it and protects it from the rain, and when the rain stops, the leaf flips over and assumes its place at its side. From that island, I took with me a large quantity of pepper and cinnamon, in exchange for coconuts. Then we passed by the Island of the 'Usrat, from which comes the Comorin aloewood, and by another island, which is a five-day journey in length and from which comes the Chinese aloewood, which is superior to the Comorin. But the inhabitants of this island are inferior to those of the first, both in their religion and in their way of life, for they are given to lewdness and wine-drinking and know no prayer nor the call to prayer. Then we came to the island of the pearl-fishers, where I gave the divers some coconuts and asked them to dive, and try my luck for me. They dived in the bay and brought up a great number of large and valuable pearls, saying, 'O master, by God, you are very lucky,' and I took everything they brought up with me to the ship.

"Then we sailed until we reached Basra, where I stayed for a few days, then headed for Baghdad. I came to my quarter, entered my house, and saluted my relatives and friends, and they congratulated me on my safety. Then I stored all the goods and gear I had brought with me, clothed the widows and the orphans, gave alms, and bestowed gifts on my relatives, friends, and all those dear to me. God had given me fourfold what I had lost, and because of my gains and the great profit I had made, I forgot what had happened to me and the toil I had suffered, and resumed my association with my friends and companions."

XVI

I N PALMYRA, once the fever had broken and Robinson had
taken off for other adventures, I wondered if I'd actually been
involved in the bloody dreams that had been haunting me since
I'd woken up. Hadn't I known Queen Zenobia, the Palmyrene
princess who had taken a stand against Rome? Hadn't I been
her husband, Odenathus, killed at Emesa on the order of his
own wife?

The enigmatic city had risen from the desert. Its colonnade,
bisected on both sides by the triumphal way, was far from straight,
pivoting surprisingly a second time at the tetrapylon, which gave
onto an immense sky and a vast stretch of sand. We were navigat-
ing between eras, held captive in a dream where ghosts conversed
with each other.

I'd gone out in the morning to admire the dawn over the ruins;
an icy wind was blowing between the stones that had not yet
turned ochre, slipping under my clothes like a reptile's tongue;
then the blue night had dissolved, warmed by a blood-red light.
Caravans of merchants from Palmyra suddenly materialized at
the edge of the town: noble lords whom I mistook for the princes
of Quraysh, expecting them to be like their distant ancestors
who spoke to each other in Aramaic and dedicated the same
religion to Bel, Allat and other forgotten idols. Did Mohammed
have this past grandeur in mind when he decided to send his

troops north? And hadn't Khalid ibn al-Walid fulfilled that dream by conquering the city in the sand barely two years after the Prophet's death?

I took refuge inside the temple of Bel. In the darkness, time blurred again and the site seemed to prefigure the Ka'aba. Inside, at the far end of a large courtyard where pilgrims would gather, stood the temple, which looked exactly the same as the one in Mecca. A bas-relief on a stone depicted a camel leading men around the building. Wasn't that the Prophet's camel?

In the Holy of Holies, there was a Byzantine fresco depicting Mary, Christ's mother, near an image of Allat, a pagan goddess. Certain Muslim chronicles said that when Mohammed entered the Ka'aba, after triumphing over his enemies, he destroyed the idols but had kept an icon of Mary. Four centuries before the Prophet's birth, the annual pilgrimage to Palmyra bore unsettling similarities to that to Mecca. The Arabs had a good memory for rituals.

This faith was also symbolized in Palmyra by those tall tombs erected in the middle of the desert, like sentries guarding an exemplary past. You only had to explore them in the sunshine to appreciate their sense of presence.

Inside the mausoleums, carved sarcophagi depicted dead families, showing the patriarch sitting in majesty and surrounded by his wife and children. These were even more impressive than the images painted over some of the burial compartments depicting the souls being carried by a bird towards a cerulean sky. They were happily letting the dove take them to a rapturous Empyrean, like those stylites in the grip of their visions.

I was glad that Thamara, a strong, dignified woman, came with me on this visit, otherwise I'd have been lost, ensnared by a dream, mixing up beliefs and gathering up all the men and women of the world in the same net. In this poetic order, Mohammed might well be an incarnation of Christ or a Nabataean priest with magic powers.

Palmyra was reborn from the desert like a phoenix, spreading its bright wings.

Zenobia became one with the Queen of Sheba in the same sacred dance. Again the processions circled a temple dedicated to a single God and his daughters, born from a verse inspired by the Devil.

We entered Bosra through the Gate of the Wind. The whole town was a field of ruins. The inhabitants lived in houses built from the stones of the ancient city. We were struck by the villagers' poverty: the children were badly dressed and miserable. The walls were black, the Roman columns looked like a forest that had burnt down. The town had been covered in charcoal, and yet the place exuded a strange, deadly beauty.

I'd imagined a dazzling town filled with light, but the colours of this place had gradually disappeared, like a badly fixed photograph, and its outlines had blurred, leaving behind nothing but shadows. It had become a Garaguz shadow theatre, like the one we saw in a café in Damascus behind the Great Mosque, a distant reflection of the Ottoman presence. Exhausted by our long journey, during which the power of the things we'd seen was as blinding as the sun on sand, we felt as though we were turning into shadows in a distant town of the past, black as the night which, for all that, was filled with illustrious spectres: the monk Buhayra, Abu Talib and the young Mohammed, who'd been welcomed as the Messiah by those strange monks, one of whom had assumed the name of a small sea which Sinbad, my oriental double, might once have sailed.

I'd been struck by the black hue of the town. I'd imagined it to be red like Palmyra or perhaps ochre. It was dark and volcanic, the stone had burned in the sun and the blackness created disturbing depths.

177

I visited the huge theatre, which was still a marvel of barbaric magnificence. You could easily lose yourself in the corridors, like catacombs where the gladiators used to lie dying. I became one of those men dazed by the light and the loud shouts of the crowd. I was the martyr devoured by the savage lions of Syria, by the lynxes, their fur sodden with blood; and the panthers' eyes held me spellbound, before engulfing me in darkness. I was a *tableau vivant* offered up for the enlightenment of the believer. I'd never see Vitalia again and my youth was lying there, dead on the stage of this amphitheatre. I know you're expecting to be told about other adventures, other mysteries and other women. There aren't any more. It's over. After Bosra, I went to Beirut, but it's too painful to tell you about that. That was where I experienced war and the death of my last, true love in a bombing raid by the Israeli army. Thamara died in my arms, broken and battered, and I returned to Carthago. End of story. It is this world I'm talking about, my noble lord, and none other. If you want to destroy it, please be my guest. I'm begging you, though, for the love of Allah, don't come up with anything else in its place.

XVII

S INBAD HAD FINISHED relating his adventures and he was aware that his guest was tired, so he tiptoed out of the room to avoid waking the strange, unfriendly dog. He knew for a fact that the beast never slept. Those animals only feigned sleep to deceive their enemies. Sinbad could sense the wariness of the vile creature that had devoured the taxi driver.

In his mind's eye, he again saw the wild animal pounce on its prey and consume the man as if there were no better food in the world. No doubt about it, the man had said some terrible things, but had he deserved such a harsh sentence and punishment? Who in Carthago was innocent or guilty? Who in the world, in fact? No one. The answer made him feel like laughing. *No one*. Wasn't that how the Sleeper had introduced himself?

The Sleeper stayed awake after Sinbad left. He'd slept for too long in his Cave for all those centuries. Sleep had deserted him. He waited in vain in the dark, but he lay there with his eyes open, not thinking or dreaming, listening to the breathing of his dog. Then he heard it no more. He never would again.

The door of his room opened. A shadow slipped in and came over to his bed.

"Why have you come back?" she asked him. "I thought you'd forgotten. Or, better still, that you were dead."

The Sleeper didn't know how to reply. He didn't remember.

"You're older than me! Older than everything here."

Lalla Fatima made a sweeping gesture with her hand at the walls of the room, from floor to ceiling, as if she actually meant the whole world.

"Everything. The town, the country. Nothing was here before you came into the world."

"I remember some things."

Memories so hazy that he sensed the lie beneath his own words. He had a premonition that everything he'd seen since his return—the town, the streets and the people, even Sinbad and Lalla Fatima—had been shadows from another life, before his long sleep, and they were coming back, not to haunt him, as he might have thought, but to show him the way to go. Naturally, he was totally in the dark about the road he had to take, about his mission, his destiny. He understood that he hadn't come back for nothing, that his dog hadn't regained its strength in vain. If he couldn't sleep, there had to be a reason for it.

"Leave my grandson alone!"

"You mean Sinbad?"

"Yes, that's exactly who I mean. You and your dog have to leave him in peace! He's innocent. He's already lost everything. He's a broken man."

"Everyone is guilty."

"You've come here for revenge. I know that. You want to shed our blood to avenge what you believe was a betrayal. It isn't my fault they captured you!"

Lalla Fatima drew herself up straighter: her hair was not so white, her shoulders not so narrow and her back not so bowed. Her steel-blue eyes sparkled again, her nipples showed beneath her blouse like those of a teenage girl, and her skin tautened, becoming as smooth and soft as it had been at the start.

The Sleeper didn't understand what she meant with all this talk of betrayal and revenge, but he felt he was involved. He was the man she'd handed over to his enemies. In a moment of weakness, torn apart by her maternal feelings, she'd sacrificed her one true love.

"They had my father. They'd tortured him. They were going to kill him and take my daughter, Amel, God rest her soul, if I didn't tell them something! So I gave them your name. And they captured you and dragged you away. I thought they had killed you. The paratroopers left and were replaced by other soldiers. We thought they were different. They didn't wear the same uniform. They spoke our language, but they were the same as the others. You were dead, you understand, and I was as young and fresh as a spring flower. My breasts hurt, my belly was grumbling with hunger. I took a man who looked like you."

Her cheeks were burning and she'd become as young as he remembered her. She had walked over to his bed, kneeled down and had stroked his face. She was twenty or maybe forty, but she was certainly no longer an old woman: Lalla Fatima was a budding flower whose petals were just opening.

"They took him as well. They were worse than their predecessors. They behaved just like them. They raped and murdered just like them. They put out the light that had been lit when the French left. They killed my husband and left me all alone with my daughter, Sinbad's mother. That's when I understood—I was paying my debt for abandoning you to the paratroopers. There are consequences if you sacrifice your first love. Look at what those bastards have done to their country. They've cast it into the fire in return for gold, black gold, which, I know without a doubt, brings only destruction and death. Like my life… which is in ruins, like this town… Carthago… Carthago… I'd never heard that name before, but it's an accurate one. It's the name of this monstrosity."

She'd unfastened her dress. He caressed the young woman's breasts, her belly, her thighs, her cunt. She rose above him, naked as the moon, and straddled him. He felt an inner stirring, his cock quickened and shifted between his legs, standing hard and long as a day of torment. Lalla Fatima mounted him like a mare, she reared so wildly and violently that it hurt a little, galloping through the flames of memory, her buttocks spread, her thighs dripping. The sound of her breathing filled the room where Dog was sleeping, her breath swept across his face, the face of an ageless man held captive by an unknown woman, similar to all women, able to take on all forms, a woman whose changeable, yet unchanging, truth was shown to him as it died with him.

Dog never slept. He never took his eyes off his master, Ooourugarri. Dog didn't like the Other, Sinnnbaaad, as he'd heard him called. Sinnnbaaad. Dog growled when he heard him, smelt him, he didn't like his Sea smell, his smell of salt and sweat. Dog also didn't like the old creature who smelled of earth and dust. Her voice sounded unpleasant to Dog's ear. It was a voice like a trickle of water about to run dry, a voice on the verge of stopping. If he'd been allowed, Dog would already have eaten Sinnnbaaad and the old creature who smelled of dry earth and rust. But Ooourugarri didn't want him to, had not ordered him to. He still obeyed his master because Ooourugarri was stronger than him. Dog submitted to Ooourugarri, Dog respected he who was the stronger and, more than anything, Dog, who had experienced Hell, didn't want to go back there for devouring Ooourugarri. He didn't like the smell down there, in the Shadows. The smell of absence, or the absence of smell: hell for Dog; and also the absence of Light, just noise, deafening noise, the noise of rodents gnawing bones. Dog didn't remember it very clearly now. He had no memory, or very little, he relied on his instincts, a mass of fleeting impressions, frightening or soothing gestures, pleasant or not so pleasant smells, which were always very interesting. Dog had been removed from the Shadows and had found himself in the Cave which wasn't much brighter. But Dog could see there. He could see the Seven Sleepers and watch over them as he'd been told to do before he'd left the Shadows. He watched over each one of them and when one finally woke after his long sleep, a sleep lasting such an eternity that Dog lost count of the years, Dog split into two and one part of Dog followed him outside, while another part stayed with the remaining Sleepers. This division felt strange to Dog, leaving him in the Cave while another Dog, a Dog identical to Dog, romped in the Light. Eventually, the divisions stopped and Ooourugarri's Dog was the last, the Collector. Yes. Dog still had a mission that no one knew. Dog was the Gatherer of legend, but Ooourugarri didn't know that or didn't seem to know. Dog wasn't sure. The master was mighty even though he thought that he was growing weaker with the Traveller, who smelled of salt and sweat. When the Time came, Dog would summon the Others, the Six Dogs. They would run to him and they would prepare to fall upon their last supper. Dog licked his chops in advance. That would definitely be the Dogs' last supper, the Kill. But before that long-awaited day, that glorious day for Dog, he had to put up with Sinnnbaaad and the old creature who smelled of dust and earth, and let them approach Ooourugarri. He had seen her coming, an ancient cloud of unbearable dust, a cloak of earth and death, to cover his master, who had stripped off his clothes to welcome Mut the fearsome, who could wield all the powers of seduction by taking on the shape of a young woman smelling of apples and fish, but who was, after all, and Dog knew it, the last refuge for maggots. Mut had risen, had covered his master with her body and Dog had growled at the danger. But Ooourugarri had raised his hand and had caressed her and Dog had fallen silent. Dog was a good dog. Dog was starving and was looking forward to the Day of Gathering.

PUSHKIN PRESS

Pushkin Press was founded in 1997. Having first rediscovered European classics of the twentieth century, Pushkin now publishes novels, essays, memoirs, children's books, and everything from timeless classics to the urgent and contemporary.

Pushkin Paper books, like this one, represent exciting, high-quality writing from around the world. Pushkin publishes widely acclaimed, brilliant authors such as Stefan Zweig, Antoine de Saint-Exupéry, Antal Szerb, Paul Morand and Hermann Hesse, as well as some of the most exciting contemporary and often prize-winning writers, including Pietro Grossi, Héctor Abad, Filippo Bologna and Andrés Neuman.

Pushkin Press publishes the world's best stories, to be read and read again.

*